Mystery at the Bookstore

ABOUT THE AUTHOR

Harleen Jaggi was born in New Delhi, India. She is now settled in California, USA. She received her early education in India where she obtained a Master's degree in Biochemistry. She continued her education after her migration to US and ended up with a Master in Clinical Sciences. Writing is her passion. She commands a simple, direct and engrossing style of story telling.

MYSTERY AT THE BOOKSTORE

The senseless murder of a poor defenseless cleaning woman has thrown the entire hitherto sleepy little Pacific coast town of Mayhaven into a deep frenzy. Fury and tension are saturating the air as people fear that a maniac killer is running loose among them, and waiting for his next opportunity to strike. The police too are baffled, as apparently there are hardly any motives or clues to go by. However, a group of four friends or "The Brave Group of Four," as they came to be known subsequently unravelled the mystery and nailed the culprits.

The Singh Family Series

Mystery at the Bookstore

By

Harleen Jaggi

Edited By

Gurcharan S. Ahluwalia

Booksmart Publications

Mission Viejo, California

ISBN-13 978-0-9790896-1-9

Copyright © 2007 by Harleen Jaggi.

Published by Booksmart publications,

PO Box 4774, Mission Viejo California 92690 USA.

www.booksmartpublications.com

Printed in the United States of America

Printed by Sir Speedy, Tustin, California USA.

Phone: (714) 832 6651

Library of Congress Control Number: 2006908749

First Edition February 2007

Contents

CHAPTER 1   1
ONE RAINY DAY

CHAPTER 2   17
THE SINGH FAMILY

CHAPTER 3   31
A PARTY ON THE PORCH

CHAPTER 4   51
DETECTIVE TRACER TALKS TO SONNY

CHAPTER 5   69
AT CHÂTEAU PEARSON

CHAPTER 6   91
AN UNCLAIMED KEY RING

CHAPTER 7   105
SLEUTHS AT THE MUSEUM

CHAPTER 8   123
AN UNPLEASANT ENCOUNTER

CHAPTER 9   139
TELL TALE PHOTOS

CHAPTER 10   149
A NOCTURNAL ADVENTURE

CHAPTER 11   161
MEETING AT MIDNIGHT

CHAPTER 12   171
PIECES FALL INTO PLACE

CHAPTER 1

One Rainy Day

On Friday morning, a tropical storm began rolling into Mayhaven, a small town on the Pacific coast. The storm brought with it strong winds and overcast skies. The ominously dark purple sky and piercing gusts of icy wind presaged the approach of a violent thunderstorm. The daily weather reports had warned of high winds and intense rain, which might extend to early the next day. Mercifully, the skies should be clearing by late Saturday.

Boris Ivanhoe, hurrying to his store, bore the brunt of the storm's brute force. The winds assaulted him relentlessly and made it hard for him to move forward. A sudden blast of cold air cut across his face, making him wince. He pulled his scarf over his ears and nose to keep out the cold. He put his freezing hands back into the pockets of his windbreaker and continued walking briskly towards his store. A garbage truck at the end of the street was making its usual weekly pickup. In spite of the inclement weather, everything seemed normal.

"Privet, Boris," saluted Sally, the twelve-year-old daughter of Jim, the owner of the neighboring Good Luck Coffee Shop. She had been sitting inside the shop, just like every other morning, waiting for her friend Amanda and her mother, who were giving her a ride to school. When she had seen

Boris, she'd rushed out of the shop to greet him; however, she quickly retreated into the shop when hit by gusts of bitingly cold air.

"Privet, Sally," he said through the door she held open in spite of the weather. Boris was smiling as he returned Sally's greeting. He had taught her that privet means hello in Russian. He was only ten years old when he migrated to the States from Russia twenty-five years earlier, and privet was one of the few Russian words he still remembered although he was unsure of its correct application and enunciation.

Boris hurried past the coffee shop, savoring the wonderfully delicious aroma of freshly brewed coffee and recently baked bagels and bread. The inviting fragrances always give an added lift to a person's spirits, especially on a day like this, thought

Boris as he turned right at the end of the street to walk towards his store.

Boris smiled again when he saw the sign in front of his store: Kanega Books and Music. He picked up his pace when he felt a raindrop on his nose. When he reached his store, he noted that the front door was slightly ajar.

"Strange!" he thought. "Gloria always keeps the door locked until opening time."

Gloria Solis was the part-time help who cleaned the place in the mornings before the store opened for business. Boris noticed, as he pushed the door open, that the sign on the door still read CLOSED. Normally, Gloria would unlock the door and change the sign to OPEN, just before Boris's expected arrival time.

Boris pushed the door open and entered the store. Ding-dong! Chimed the bell merrily, as it did every time someone opened the door.

Boris had recently installed this bell. He looked at the clock on the wall. It was 8:25. Because he was late, he was expecting to meet a flustered Gloria complaining about his tardiness. However, to his surprise and relief she was not at the door. Maybe she was not yet finished with her chores. He looked around for Gloria but didn't see her. Usually, she was through with her chores before he came in at 8:00 a.m. I owe her an apology, thought Boris. He changed the sign on the door to OPEN.

The store was exceedingly quiet, which was unusual. Usually Gloria would be making lot of clamor bustling around finishing last of her chores putting away the vacuum, duster, mop and buckets. Today there was no sound except the storm's wail as it rushed over the mountainous terrain outside. Boris saw the newspapers lying next to the door and glanced back at the news stand. It was still displaying yesterday's editions. He frowned. It was unlike Gloria not to replace the newspapers in the newspaper stand. Boris looked around for her again. He did not see her, but he did see a few books knocked down from the corner shelf. Where is Gloria? Something was seriously amiss. Boris brushed the feeling aside as he picked up the books and put them back on the shelf.

He was carrying a colorful ethnic-looking shoulder bag, which contained his lunch and umbrella. He put the bag behind the cashier counter that also served as his desk. The counter was situated in the centre of the back wall of the store. He could watch almost the entire store from his desk, including the customers as they entered and left the store.

The area between the front door

and cashier desk was clear. There were bookshelves on either side, but the middle of the room was kept clear so customers could stand comfortably while waiting their turn to be served.

Boris could smell fresh coffee. Gloria always had a fresh pot going. Boris offered coffee free of charge to his customers until 10:00 a.m. This was good for business, as many times a passerby was tempted to enter the store for a free cup of coffee and ended up buying a newspaper or a magazine.

He noticed something missing. It was odd that Gloria had forgotten to place his morning cup of coffee and the day's newspaper on his desk, as she did every morning. Gloria had been providing this service to Boris of her own volition, as it was not part of her specific duties. Today she had clearly forgotten. He let the strange feeling pass for the moment and bent down under the desk to turn on the cameras. They had a warm-up time of five minutes. Ding-dong! Went the store bell once again.

Boris stood up and saw a well-dressed, medium-built, bespectacled man with thinning gray hair and a middle age spread standing at the door. The man was shaking water off his expensive leather jacket. It was raining torrentially outside. The man looked perturbed and seemed to be unsure about whether to stay or leave.

"Good morning, sir," hailed Boris. "How can I help you?"

"Good morning," responded the bespectacled man in a polished but reserved tone with a hint of a stammer. "Sorry to bother you so early in the morning. I came to see...I mean...talk to Gloria."

"I don't know where she is at the moment. I have just arrived and have not seen her so far. It's very unlike her to have left, leaving the door open. Maybe she has just stepped out for a moment and will turn up shortly."

"Well, my name is Ernest, Ernest Pearson," the man introduced himself. "Gloria is an employee at Mayhaven's World Discovery Museum on the weekends. Today is her day off, but I came to see if she could work overtime today. The other cleaning person has called in sick and the place does need sprucing up before it opens today."

Boris was taken by surprise. He knew about Dr. Pearson, a premier dignitary of the town. He was reported to be fabulously rich and a go-getter by nature. It was therefore strange that he should come personally looking for Gloria. He could have sent any of his minions or could have called.

Boris kept the thought to himself and said, "Glad to meet you in person, Dr. Pearson. Everyone in Mayhaven knows you, as well as the service you are providing to the community. I know that Gloria works for you too. She is a devoted and unobtrusive worker. She is certain to turn up. By the way, are you contemplating some further additions to the museum? I saw some trucks come in last weekend." Boris was trying to pass the time by engaging in polite conversation as he walked around getting the store ready for opening.

A shadow crossed Ernest's face, but it was gone so quickly that Boris was certain he'd imagined it. In fact he was aware that Ernest was smiling at him. "Oh, yes! I'm

planning to add a theatre to the museum.
Then we can have exclusive space to host
exhibitions without causing any disturbance
to the existing displays. Construction plans
for the additions have been approved,
but the actual work will begin around the
middle of next year. The changes I expect
will prove to be a big draw, adding greatly to
the convenience of the visitors. Currently,
I have the 'Kites from Around the World'
exhibition, which opens today. That's why I'm
expecting a big crowd on the weekend and
had come to see if Gloria could work today."

Boris had been to the museum a few
times. He liked the idea of the addition of
a new theatre. "I agree that the provision
of a theatre would be a step in the right
direction," he responded. "With additional
space available, would you consider the

possibility of adding a permanent stand for sale of museum-related books and souvenirs? That would bring in extra income for the museum. I could set it up for you."

Ernest nodded in agreement. "It's an excellent suggestion. Maybe we could explore it further at a later time." He looked towards the store door as if hoping Gloria would be there.

Boris also looked around yet again. By now he was wondering if Gloria had left but forgotten to lock the store first. However, just to be sure that she was not in the back, he started to walk towards the back of the store along with Ernest.

"The problems never come alone," quipped Ernest. "They come in droves. Here I am on the verge of opening an important exhibition and my cleaning help has taken ill. God knows for how long. Then

Joseph, who doubles as my housekeeper and museum caretaker, has just told me that he will be unable to come to work for the next few days. That's life I guess."

The store bell chimed again. Boris turned around and saw a woman enter the store with two kids. She went to the stationery stand. Boris was obliged to go and take care of the customers. He therefore excused himself to Ernest saying, "Let me take care of these customers. You are more than welcome to wait here for Gloria. Help yourself to a cup of coffee."

Just then, two more customers entered the store: a woman with a turquoise beaded scarf and a man with a wooden leg. The man picked up a newspaper, paid for it, poured a cup of coffee and walked out. The kids chose the stationery items they needed and left after their mother paid.

The woman with the beaded scarf wanted to look at birthday cards for her mother. Boris pointed across the store. The cards were on a shelf against the left wall of the store, near the music section and behind all the bookshelves—the one area of the store that Boris could not watch directly from the desk. As the woman walked towards the card section, Boris glanced at the screen of his camera. He observed something on the floor near the card stand. Boris zoomed in on the spot and saw an object that looked like a foot. His eyes widened. Heart pounding, he further scanned the spot with added magnification. Lo, there was Gloria lying on the floor.

He ran towards the card rack where the woman in the turquoise scarf had started screaming. Dr. Pearson

came running towards them. They found
Gloria lying in a pool of blood.

Boris noticed that the sign on the door still read CLOSED.

CHAPTER 2

The Singh Family

It was a bright, sunny Sunday. The Singh family had just returned from Gurudwara, which literally means Guru's (master's) house. It's a house of prayer for the Sikhs. Sikhs belong to a budding religious denomination hailing predominately from Punjab, a state of India. The Sikh religion promotes the concept of one God. It recognizes God as Creator, Sustainer and Destroyer of the universe. A true Sikh is always alive to the reality of the Lord and leads a chaste life.

He earns his living through honest work and
willingly shares the fruit of his labor with
the needy and less privileged. Like all other
faiths, Sikhism also inculcates the need to
adopt a pious way of life, resolutely curbing
such failings as lust, greed, anger and pride.

Guru Nanak, a master seer of his times,
founded the Sikh faith around the turn of
the fourteenth century. The faith was further
nurtured by nine gurus who followed Guru
Nanak over a period of two hundred years.
Guru Arjun Dev, the fifth guru of the Sikhs,
compiled the scriptures of the Sikh faith into
a book form. The finished book reverently
designated as Guru Granth Sahib includes
compositions of the Sikh gurus and a number
of other like-minded saints and seers of the
time. Essentially, the Granth provides a unique
treasury of melodious hymns, which extol the

grandeur of the Lord and seek His blessing for peace, prosperity and enlightenment.

Dr. Darshan Singh and his wife Anu Kaur are devout Sikhs. They had migrated to the United States some seventeen years ago and have two children: a fourteen-year-old son, Shawn Singh, and an eleven-year-old daughter, Jasmine Kaur. Dr. Darshan Singh is a professional physician. He had opened his clinic in Mayhaven soon after his arrival in the States. The local population holds him in high esteem for his ethical dealing and caring nature.

"Daddy, you promised we would fly kites today after we return from Gurudwara," demanded dark-eyed, dark-haired Jasmine. She knew that Daddy could not refuse her request because she had behaved like an angel at the Gurudwara. She was excitedly anticipating flying her Tinker Bell kite.

"I'll help," volunteered Shawn, her brother, who was also dark-haired and dark-eyed. They raced down to the garage to get the kites. Darshan joined them a moment later.

"Hey, Jasmine! You are back already. Can you play?" asked Holly sweetly. Holly Akers and her brother Jordan Akers were friends with Shawn and Jasmine. Unlike Shawn and Jasmine, both Jordan and Holly had blond hair and blue-green eyes. The Singhs and the Akers lived next door to each other. The Akers kids had been waiting for the Singh kids since morning. They knew that the Singh family always went to the Gurudwara on Sunday morning.

"We're flying kites with Daddy today," answered Jasmine excitedly. "You are welcome to join us. Is that okay, Daddy?"

"Sure, Holly," said Darshan as he tied the string to the kite. Holly ran to get her kite. The weather was perfect for kite flying.

Jasmine's kite was made of a light wood framework and covered with a light synthetic material. It was pink with a green Tinker Bell and a pink and green tail. Holly had a red dragon kite with a red and yellow tail.

A few minutes later, Shawn was helping Jasmine get her kite into the air. "Jasmine, you hold the line and I'll hold the kite. When I release the kite, it will go right up. Do not pull back the kite but let it fly away from you, and then, as it floats, pull in on the line gently. Repeat, pulling on the line and letting the kite float a little, a few times till the kite gains the height and finds a good steady wind current."

"Roger that," said Jasmine.

Jasmine had her kite up after a few

false starts. By that time, Darshan had also helped Holly get her kite into air.

"Shawn, did you know kite flying is a popular pastime and a competitive sport in India, especially in northern parts like Punjab?" said Darshan . "During spring season, special competitions are held. Kites are elaborately designed and decorated. Contestants take their kites to the highest point in the sky and let the kites ride there for some time. Kite-fighting contests are also held in which competitors maneuver their kites to attack and cut loose the kites of their opponents."

"A kite-flying competition!" said Shawn. "I would love to see that in the Olympics."

"What would you like to see in the Olympics?"

Everyone turned to see Detective

Edward Tracer sauntering over with a widening grin. The lanky forty-eight-year-old detective had just alighted from his car. Detective Edward Tracer, also known as Eddy to his friends and associates, was the detective in charge of the special crime division of the Mayhaven police station. A close friend of the Singh's, Detective Tracer was extremely popular with the children too.

"Hello, Detective Tracer," said Shawn, Jasmine, Holly and Dr. Singh in one voice, which made everyone laugh.

"Hello, Darshan. Shawn." said Edward as he waved heartily to the girls. "Today is a perfect day for kite flying. There is a 'Kites from Around the World' exhibition going on at the World Discovery Museum."

"Is that so? Well, kites have become increasingly popular all over the world, including Australia, Switzerland and South Africa. Kite flying used to be a simple and inexpensive hobby, but nowadays kites are also being used for aerial photography and other scientific studies." Darshan had been a kite-flying expert from a very young age.

"When I was a kid, I could spend endless hours running in the breeze with a homemade paper and bamboo kite," said Edward.

"These days, you can choose to spend your money on a strong stunt or power kite that will pull you along or may even lift you off your feet if the wind current is strong enough," said Darshan. "Markets are carrying an expanding variety of kites fashioned in the shapes of birds, fish or dragons. There are also kites equipped with whistles or pipes that emit musical sounds as the wind blows through them.

"There is a flip side too," Darshan
continued. "Kite flying is not all about gaiety
and good cheer. Occasionally, it also results
in grievous accidents leading to loss of
limbs or even life. In order to gain additional
height, lads and lasses in India and other
neighboring countries are often tempted to
fly their kites from the rooftops. When the
kites are afloat high in the air, they not only
have to keep their eyes focused on the kite
but simultaneously ambulate to and fro to
maintain the height of the kite and prevent
the kite from suddenly floundering down.
Often in this blind ambulation, a person can
unwittingly step over the edge of the roof and
fall to the ground. As a precaution, parents
started putting up parapets on the rooftops.
But then, who has succeeded in separating a
youth from his follies. The young enthusiasts

started mounting these parapets to give their kites the benefit of the added height. As a result, the kite-related accidents became even more sinister. The concern for preventing such mishaps is reflected in the embargo placed on kite flying by some countries."

Just then, Jordan, Holly's brother, came and joined the fun. Jordan and Shawn were good friends. Jordan was tall and slim and had recently got into bodybuilding. He aspired to be a physician and specialize in genetics. However, Shawn was into technology and computers. His idol was Bill Gates.

"Shawn, check out my iPod," said Jordan. "My dad gave it to me for my birthday last week."

"Sweet! Let me see it. What songs you have? Let me listen." Shawn took the white rectangular iPod from Jordan.

"I just got it. I have not had time to put music. Do you know how?"

"That's easy," said Shawn. "Let's go do it."

"Wait a minute, Shawn," said Jordan. "I want to show you my muscles. I've been working out regularly these days." Jordan took off his shirt and proceeded to flex his biceps. "Touch here. Hard as rock, aren't they?"

"Jordan!" Shouted a horrified Holly. "Put your shirt on. Nobody wants to see your stinky blubber." Everyone turned to look at Jordan, who turned completely red as they all started laughing. He put his shirt on.

Shawn and Jordan ran into the house. They stopped in the kitchen to grab a few sugarcoated brownies from the brownie jar, as well as glasses of milk.

"Hi, Mrs. Singh," said Jordan when

he saw Anu in the kitchen. Anu, a trim, pleasant, attractive woman with warm brown eyes, was a homemaker. She turned around and saw the iPod in Jordan's hand.

"Hi, Jordan," said Anu. "What's that in your hand?" Anu was always interested in what Shawn, Jasmine and their friends were doing.

"iPod, my birthday present from my dad," answered Jordan.

Shawn didn't like it when his mom was nosy but he did'nt say anything instead he reminded his mom that his birthday was coming up, "Mom, can I have an iPod for my birthday too?"

"Oki doki. I will put that on the list too and you can pick one item for your birthday from that list," said Anu.

Shawn and Jordan ran up the stairs as Anu got busy frying samosa, a traditional Indian snack made of a spicy potato and peas mixture, which was then ensconced into pastry dough sheets and deep-fried. Her mind was still on the two-day old news of murder in the bookstore.

She knew Boris because she had volunteered at the library, once a week, a few years ago. Boris's mother had been serving as a librarian at that library for over fifteen years and the two had become friends. Anu had left a message for Detective Tracer at the station, where she also did volunteer work as a researcher for special cases. She was interested in knowing if there was an opportunity for her to do some digging into the murder in the bookstore case. But she knew that as a matter of policy, no assignments were given to volunteers in cases involving homicide.

Mayhaven is a harmonious little
hamlet along the Pacific Coast

CHAPTER 3

A Party on the Porch

Darshan and Edward, still talking about the kites, moved to the porch at the front entrance of the Singh residence and sat down on the bamboo chairs with flowered cushions. They were watching Jasmine and Holly flying their kites when the appetizing aroma of fried samosa began to fill the air. Darshan got up and headed into the house.

"Anu, Eddy is here!" said Darshan a bit loudly as he walked towards the kitchen. "We will need tea with your always-yummy samosas. I'll make the tea."

"I'm almost done," said Anu. "The tea is also ready. Here, you take out this tray, and I'll bring the tea." Anu handed the tray with samosas and hot and sweet tamarind sauce to Darshan. "Thank you for your offer to make tea. I'll take a rain check on it."

Out on the porch, Dr. Singh set the tray on the bamboo table with a glass top. Detective Edward admired Singh's cactus garden, which contained numerous varieties of cacti and succulents. The cacti garden added a high point to the fascinating view.

"Hello, Ed." Anu greeted detective Edward as she wheeled the tea trolley onto the porch.

"Hello Anu," said Detective Edward. Anu sat down on the chair next to Darshan and said to Darshan, "I thought you were going to spend the afternoon flying kites with Jasmine."

"Look!" Darshan said defensively, "I have both Jasmine and Holly's kites floating high in the sky. Now it's up to them to keep the kites up as long as they can."

"Anu, you are a master cook," complimented Edward, biting into a steamy, crispy and spicy samosa.

"Thank you," said Anu graciously. She enjoyed cooking but enjoyed the compliments even more. "I have completed the typing assignment on stolen art objects, which is now ready for submission. You can take it with you if you like. If you need any additional information, please let me know. I'll be happy to get that as well. It was really an interesting assignment. I didn't know that art thefts were so numerous. It seems stealing art objects has become a flourishing industry in itself."

As a volunteer with the Mayhaven police station's special crime division, she worked every Tuesday from 12:30 to 4:30 p.m. Her jobs included filing of papers, data entry work and online search of information needed by detectives to bring a host of felons to justice including swindlers, burglars and drug pushers. Her latest involvement was with the field of stolen art. Anu found working with the sheriff's department highly exciting.

"Thank you, Anu, for your assistance. The station cannot run without its dedicated volunteers," quipped Detective Edward. "You are correct. Crimes such as theft, fraud, looting and trafficking of art and other cultural properties across state and international lines is an ominously burgeoning criminal enterprise, leading to very high national and

international losses. Most art heists are subtle
and involve forged documents, fake records
and spurious receipts of transactions. The
FBI has put together a new task force to take
on the problem of the global trade in stolen
art objects. The force will closely look into the
goings-on between dealers of art and antique
items and museum officials. Presently, FBI is
on the lookout for a French national who may
have entered the country illegally via the San
Diego border. FBI strongly believe that this
individual is currently in Mayhaven, seeking to
purchase religious icons stolen from Mexico."

At that point, Shawn and Jordan,
joined the group on the porch.

"Trafficking in stolen art is big business
in Latin America," added Darshan. "Thieves
break into museums, churches, convents and
shrines and steal paintings, priceless statues,

and other sacred icons of all descriptions. Each piece is worth thousand of dollars. There is always a big furor when such a piece of art or sacred relic disappears but things quiet down after a while. Time is then opportune to put such items on market."

"Wouldn't it be sacrilegious to steal statues from a place of worship?" asked Shawn incredulously, sitting on an empty chair next to Detective Tracer. "It's like plundering the home of God. Who would want to buy old art objects, especially stolen from religious places?"

Jordan also looking bewildered sat down on the empty chair next to Shawn. "I agree with Shawn. The person who would buy stolen religious art would be risking divine displeasure for being an accessory to the crime."

Everyone laughed at Shawn

and Jordan's sincere comments.

"Shawn, Jordan, please have some samosas," said Anu.

"Thank you, Mrs. Singh," said Jordan as he picked up a crispy samosa.

"Shawn, you'd be surprised," said Darshan. "All over the world, the market is excellent and expanding for these objects especially here in Southern California, Texas and Arizona where Spanish-style manor homes are popular. These objects are in demand because of their potential as solid long-term investments. Then they have what can be termed as snob value for flaunting as family heirlooms. Some take them as lucky charms, others use them as high points in house décor and, of course, they are always excellent as conversation pieces."

"But how do these pieces of art get

sold undetected?" Jordan asked animatedly, as he picked up another samosa.

"Many of the stolen art pieces resurface at flea markets and auction houses," Edward volunteered. "Reputed auction houses do not intentionally handle smuggled antiquities. But it is hard to put a finger on a tainted item in a large sized lot. Sometimes the auction houses receive large collections, accompanied by detailed and accurate documentation. But in other cases, an item may come with a reference only to the literature in which a similar object is described, or the museum in which a similar object was on display. There is no information about the origin of the piece, and the source of acquisition is also ambiguous. Then there are private collectors who will consciously look the other way if the price is right. A famous museum

in Los Angeles was recently under close
scrutiny for acquiring certain art objects from
Europe which were suspected to be stolen."

"Invariably, such objects are
insured for hefty sums of money," added
Darshan. "As such, inside frauds are
also on the rise with owners themselves
enacting fake burglaries to claim huge
compensations from insurance companies."

"It's not as if these thefts go undetected,"
said Anu. "Police also has its quota of success
stories. Recently, media went to town on
recovery of the wooden altarpiece of Saint
Francis that was stolen from a convent near
Puebla in Mexico. The piece was seized from
an art gallery in New Mexico and carried a
price tag of twenty-five thousand dollars.
The owners of the gallery did not know the
piece was stolen. They cooperated with

the police and the altarpiece was returned
to the convent in Mexico. Saint Francis is
highly venerated in Mexico and his followers
ecstatically celebrated the occasion."

"We have information that freshly stolen
art objects are being brought to Mayhaven
and stashed away for some time until things
settle down," said Edward. "As the memories
of their thefts fade from public mind, the
objects are taken out and passed on to buyers
in different territories. There are rumors
that some of the stolen sacred art objects
from the Pyramids in Egypt are stashed
somewhere in Mayhaven, and that their sale
is being negotiated with a European buyer."

"There was also recent news about
theft of some sacred relics from Mexico
and there was also an article about illegal
excavations going on in sites around

Pyramids in Egypt," chipped in Shawn, totally enthused by the topic of the conversation.

"Crime gets much too blown up by media," observed Darshan. "Radio, TV, newspapers, magazines and the internet are so focused on murder and mayhem that it makes one shiver every time one has to step outside in the street. In Mayhaven these days, media is having a field day playing up what has been termed 'murder in the bookstore.' The murder has everyone's attention diverted from all major national and international matters of concern including gasoline prices, war, hurricanes etc."

"The murder of Gloria Solis is extremely baffling." Detective Edward sounded somewhat casual, but Anu could sense the undercurrent of tension in his voice. "It's a glaringly audacious crime. There are hardly any clues or suspects. There is no evidence of any attempted robbery in the store at that time. It just has the color of a highly random killing. We have not come across any apparent motive for anyone to kill Gloria Solis. She was not young, had no money, no enmity, no rivalry...nothing. We can only speculate about Gloria. She seemed to have lived by the motto that we earn our own keep, need no favors and live life on our own terms. There are some people in the world with the mind set that they came into the world alone, and they will also go alone in the end, so why mix up with anyone in the intervening period."

"You're right," said Anu. "Gloria Solis was serene, kept to herself and led a solo life. People generally left her alone. She was a portly charwoman of Mexican descent. She had an only son, Sonny, whom she had brought up as a single parent. I am sure

Sonny would know the details about her life. He loved her a lot. She worked from six thirty to eight thirty in the morning at Kanega Books and Music, cleaning the store prior to the arrival of the owner. I met her on a few occasions when I went to the store early to pick up stationery items for my children."

"Homicide always gets centre stage in media," said Darshan. "Of course, that reflects negatively on police work. You seem to be worried a bit now but wait for accolades when you nab the culprit." He poured a cup of hot cardamom flavored tea and handed it to Detective Tracer. "The murder has taken the residents of Mayhaven by storm. Otherwise, life here flows at such a languid pace. Nothing ever seems to move. Hitherto, Gloria was a mere nonentity, but now her name is on every tongue. Newspapers are full of stories about her. Same with TV and radio. Even the hot news about trafficking in stolen sacred art from Mexico has been pushed to the background."

"Thank you for the tea," said Edward in appreciation to Anu. "It's delicious. Media is indeed putting pressure on us. There is no discernible motive and almost no positive lead. The only suspect we have is Dr. Ernest Pearson, which is neither here nor there."

"Ernest Pearson?" Exclaimed a puzzled Darshan. "Do you mean the director of Mayhaven's World Discovery Museum? No way! How could he be involved?"

Shawn was paying close attention to the conversation because the topic was really exciting. "Didn't you say that there is an exhibition of kites currently going on at the museum?" he interjected. "Do you think we can visit the museum this weekend, or Jasmine and I could bike down to the museum? It's not very far. I'd like to see the kites. It sounds interesting." He and his sister had inherited their mom's zest for excitement and adventure, as well as their father's love of kites.

"Yes, of course we can," said Anu. "Let us all go together on Friday. Your schools are closed this Friday due to teacher development day, and your dad has the day off too."

"Hey, the kites are really flying high with those novices," said Jordan loudly which made everyone look at Jasmine and Holly flying kites on the green lawn. They all smiled as they watched the girls struggling to keep the kites afloat.

"Jordan, do you want to come with us to the museum on Friday?" asked Shawn.

"Is it okay, Mrs. Singh, if I come with you?" inquired Jordan politely.

"Sure, Jordan. No problem."

"Shawn, let's go ask my mom," said Jordan excitedly.

Shawn and Jordan each picked up a samosa and ran to Jordan's house.

"Why is Dr. Pearson a suspect?" asked Anu.

"Well," said Detective Tracer, "it's unusual for someone in his position to come to a bookstore asking about cleaning help. It therefore looks strange that he should drive to the store at eight thirty in the morning to offer overtime work to Gloria. He could have easily sent any of his junior employees. The murder was committed sometime between six thirty and eight thirty. I reckon it was after seven, because Gloria had picked up the day's newspapers but had not yet placed them on the stand. Maybe, Ernest was still

in the store when Boris came. He could have
alerted the bell surreptitiously as a ploy to
give the impression that he was just entering.
Felons often make efforts to cover their tracks."
This was mere conjecturing on the detective's
part to show that nothing was impossible.

"However, this theory does not
hold water because there is no motive,"
added the detective. "What possible motive
could Ernest have for committing such a
heinous crime? His affability, generous
nature and refined personal ways stand in
stark contrast to those of murderers."

Darshan and Anu were listening
closely to the details, although they already
knew most of the story from the newspapers
and the television. However, newspapers
did not mention Ernest as their suspect.

"According to the press," said Anu, "the

newspapers were dropped in front of the store around six o'clock that day. Gloria might have picked them up as she arrived. Boris is not sure of her exact routine. But she always made coffee around seven. Gloria used to keep the store door locked till she had finished work and was ready to leave. Sometimes, if Boris came early, the door would be locked and he had to use his key to enter. One can thus easily assume that Gloria knew the killer and had unlocked the door to let him in or that the killer was already on the premises prior to her arrival. There was no evidence of any forced entry or of any struggle, even though some books had fallen from the shelf." She had been following the story with great interest.

Sipping his tea, Darshan stretched his legs, leaned back in the chair and looked at the two kites soaring majestically in the clear blue sky. It was such a beautiful sunny day after the heavy rain of the past two days.

"Incidentally, we found an envelope containing five thousand dollars taped to the underside of a coffee table during our search at Gloria's place," said Edward. "We also found an envelope containing newspaper clippings about stolen art and a book on the subject of Spanish art. The discovery of money raises quite a few suspicions. I have a feeling that the money is somehow connected to the murder."

"Well, an envelope containing money and taped to the bottom of a table does look suspicious," said Darshan. The phone started ringing. Darshan went inside to pick it up.

As if realizing he had been talking to Anu and Darshan for almost two hours, Detective Tracer excused himself, saying, "I'll be going back to the station. I had come to pick up the research report on stolen art." He picked up the folder Anu had given him, cautioning her not to forget to log the hours she spent on it. "Thank you for your hard work."

He walked into the house and waved goodbye to Darshan, who was still on the phone, and then walked off to his car briskly.

CHAPTER 4

Detective Tracer Talks to Sonny

D etective Edward Tracer walked up the steps of Gloria's two-story peach and orange house. He saw Gloria's cat sitting on the bay window and looking outside, as if waiting for her mistress to walk in through the front door. He had delayed his meeting with Gloria Solis's son, Sonny, for as long as he could. He was aware that Sonny was devastated by his mother's death. The detective wished that he had some positive news about the identity of the killer. Unfortunately the killer and the motive were still unpinned. With a deep sigh, Detective Tracer rang the bell.

Sonny opened the door slowly and greeted Edward. "Hello, Detective. Please come in. What can I do for you?"

Edward could see the deep sadness in Sonny's face. Sonny had returned to his mother's house grief-stricken. He was taken aback to find the place in total disarray because of the police search. The home of his childhood years now wore an alien look. Gloria had taken pride in always keeping her home immaculately clean and tidy. Sonny still half expected his mom to emerge from the kitchen, wiping her hands on her apron and bringing along with her the delicious aroma of Mexican food. He even missed her continuous nagging to assist her in smartening and sprucing up the place.

Her home was now unrecognizable. Police had scoured the place with a fine-tooth comb, seeking clues to unravel the mystery of the murder. Gloria's neat little writing desk was cluttered with newspapers, photographs, books, clothes and boxes. Drawers had been yanked open and their contents spilled onto the floor. Furniture was moved but not put back. Tables and chairs were upturned. Mattresses, bed linens and drapes were heaped at random.

The detectives had taken a few articles from the house that they believed could shed some light on the perplexing case. Taped to the refrigerator was the list of items they had taken, including Gloria's computer that Sonny had bought for her as Christmas gift, her mail, her filing cabinet and an envelope containing five thousand dollars in cash and clippings from newspapers about stolen art from Mexico.

Sonny knew about the money. His mother had shown the money to him when he was visiting her last weekend. She was excited and aglow. Keeping her voice low, she'd whispered, "I will have more. I will be rich." Her wrinkled face was alight with a twisted smile.

Sonny had looked at his mother and asked, "Where did you get the money, Ma?"

His mother had refused to divulge anything. She seemed to be under a spell of greed. Sonny suspected something was wrong. His mother had a hand-to-mouth existence all her life. How could she have come by such a large amount of money? He had repeatedly implored her to tell him more about the windfall, but she adamantly refrained from saying anything. She was secretive by nature and not given to sharing her confidences with

anyone. He had stormed out of the house
in a huff, hoping to make her see sense.

Now he felt guilty about getting
angry and walking out on her. Confused
and numb with grief, he was purposefully
trying to blot out the memory of the
last visit to his mother's house.

When the doorbell rang, Gloria's cat,
Patsy, was the first to spot Detective Edward
Tracer coming up the steps. She watched as
he rang the bell and Sonny opened the door.
Detective Tracer entered the house on Sonny's
invitation and was immediately assailed by a
pungent odor bordering on a nasty stench. His
sharp senses quickly made out the smells of
the Mexican spices mixed with tobacco fumes.
In all probability, the tobacco smell came from
the cigarettes smoked by the visiting police
officers. Everyone was startled when the cat

jumped from his perch to greet the visitor with a purr. Then she moved to the kitchen.

Sonny invited detective Edward to come inside and sit down. The detective sat on the chair opposite to the sofa. Sonny sat down on the sofa next to Gabriel, his three-year-old son, who was playing with his toy fire truck and watching TV. Gloria had given the biblical name to her grandson. In the Bible, Gabriel is the angel who explains the signs from God to Mary and foretells the conception, birth and mission of Jesus. Gloria adored Gabriel, or Gabe, and often called him Sonny Junior.

Sonny's wife, Mary Jane, was outside in the backyard looking at Gloria's garden of herbs and medicinal plants. There was stillness and sadness in the air. Even after the passage of five days, Mary Jane had not succeeded in getting over her grief. She dearly missed her mother-in-law, or Mama, as she used to call her affectionately. Studying the garden furniture that she and Sonny had purchased to replace the worn-out patio set tears came to her eyes as she remembered how delighted Mama had been with the gift.

Mary Jane looked around in dismay. The sunny, hot, dry weather was making life difficult. It did not seem as if it had been pouring rain less than a week ago. The plants needed watering. Mary Jane turned on the water, picked up the garden hose, and started watering the plants.

Meanwhile Detective Tracer, was looking around at the disarray in the living room. It seemed a fierce tornado had swept through the house. He looked at Sonny and said "I am very sorry about your loss. Please be assured that we will do our best to nail the killer and please do bear with us and give us some time. We will also request that you do share with us any information you may have that could help us close in on the criminals. Presently, we do not have even a clue about the motive that could prompt someone to commit such a despicable act. Once we are able to establish the motive, we will get the needed lead to trace and book the bastards."

At that point, Mary Jane walked into the room. Detective Edward turned to her. "Hello, Mary Jane. I was just assuring Sonny that we will pursue the case relentlessly and will not relax until we lay our hand on the wretches who did this. We may not have many leads yet, but a murderer always leaves a bloody trail in the wake. We are looking for help from all the quarters. We cannot afford to let a killer remain at large for a long time because one who has killed once will surely kill again."

"Please count me in," responded Mary Jane spontaneously. "I too will do anything to assist you. Gloria was such a dear. She should get justice. I miss her a lot. Gloria was my mama too. She cared a lot for Sonny, Gabe and me."

Edward asked Sonny if Gloria was facing any personal problems at home or at work.

Sonny did not know of any. "I don't know why anyone would want to kill my mom. She was harmless. She had very few close friends, but then she had no staunch enemies either. She was God-fearing, regular churchgoer and always willing to volunteer for different community projects. A devout follower of Saint Francis, she was even keeping a statue of the saint in her house. That's why I'm baffled by the police theory that the killer was known to Gloria, and that he had gone to the store with the sole intent of murdering her."

"Sonny, I do not want to upset you, but the police have given consideration to the fact that there was no sign of forced entry into the store, no sign of any fight or struggle, and no sign of theft or burglary."

"I really have no clue. Mom had a very reserved nature. She mostly kept to herself. She did not have much faith in people, particularly from the time my dad walked out on her. When I was growing up, she would not let me make any close friends, lest I too leave her. She believed that people were manipulative, their loyalty always fickle. I recently had been trying to persuade her that she should get over this fear and take things easy. But there was no way to reason with her."

"So she had no one close to her other than you and Mary Jane?" said Edward.

"Well, other than us, she was also very close to Tia Ally Zeballos, who lives in Mexico. Tia and Mama often talked for a long time on the phone. Their conversations covered almost everything in life: family, gossip, local politics, health problems... Talking with Tia Ally helped Mama forget her worries and tensions a bit. I have informed her about Mama's death, and she will be arriving in a day or two. Tia Ally said that she will be bringing with her a sealed envelope that my mom had entrusted to her care some time ago. Ma had instructed her to give the envelope to me, should anything happen to her. Ma had told her not to open the envelope herself."

Sonny paused, looking out of the window as if another thought had occurred to him. He turned to Edward and continued. "I see your point that the killer might be known to my mama. But then we have such a small circle in which everyone knows everyone else. I cannot imagine anyone we know of committing such a heinous crime." Sonny stopped as if fighting back tears.

Mary Jane put an arm around her husband and quietly picked up the thread from where he had left off. "Mama was the worrying type. She particularly worried about health matters. She possessed a wealth of information about medicinal herbs and plants and their uses. When she was at home, she would always be busy brewing different decoctions for curing one ailment or the other. She took great care of not only her health but ours also. She was always giving us advice on what to eat, what to avoid, and how to follow a strict regime of daily exercise. Besides her regular job at the museum, she also took up part-time work that helped her pay her bills. She was always dreaming about going back to Mexico and living with Tia Ally after her retirement, but that was not to be."

Edward had been taking rapid notes of what Sonny and Mary Jane were saying. "I'd like to meet Tia Ally when she arrives and examine the contents of the envelope. It may hold the key to this mystery. Do you know about the money? We found an envelope containing five thousand dollars and newspaper clippings of stolen art objects from churches in Mexico. The envelope was taped to the underside of the coffee table in the family room."

"What money?" asked Sonny, looking puzzled. "She was hinting that she would soon be rich and may not have to work for the rest of her life. But I had only laughed, thinking she was saying it to make me comfortable." Sonny got up, walked to the window and gazed at the horizon.

Sensing that the interview had come to an abrupt end, Edward took the hint and started to wrap things up. However, he could not shake the feeling that there was something about Gloria and the money that Sonny was not willing to share.

"Do you know of anything more that can shed some additional light on this crime?" Edward asked Sonny.

Sonny turned towards the detective and said, "No, I have already told you all I know. I have concealed nothing. I am worried that my mother's name may get sullied through any unfounded insinuations."

Gabe started crying, and
Mary Jane picked up her son.

Edward wanted to ask a few more
question, especially about the money, but
he refrained, thinking that it was not an
opportune time to pursue the matter further.
Besides, Gabe was crying even harder.

"Is it all right if I come back
again in a day or two to get a few more
elaborations?" asked Edward.

"Yes please, that would
be fine," agreed Sonny.

Edward let himself out and walked
down the steps to the driveway. He
was about to get into his car when he
was accosted from behind.   "Detective,
can I talk to you for a minute?"

Edward turned to face a woman
with a sparse build. She was wearing a

crisp, blue flowered tunic, round metal glasses and black loafers. Her hair was tied in a tight bun on top of her head.

"Hello, Detective. My name is Hannah Prye. I am a next-door neighbor of Gloria's. Prye is my last name only," Hannah said with a short self-conscious laugh. "I am not at all a nosy bitch snooping around other people's affairs. So do not be taken in by my name."

Edward nodded in understanding and Hannah continued.

"Anyways, I have to get something off my chest," said Hannah saucily. "Gloria and I were neighbors but we rarely talked. I saw Sonny coming to visit his mother a day prior to her murder. The visit did not go well. There was a big commotion in their house. I heard a lot of loud arguing. Sonny was highly angry with Gloria which was very unlike him. He adored his mom. Gloria had worked hard all her life and had sacrificed a lot to bring him up as a single parent."

"I went to the window and listened to what was going on. I know that it is impolite and unethical to eavesdrop on other people, and I am not in the habit of doing so. But that commotion was acting like a powerful magnet and I could not contain myself."

Edward looked at her quizzically but without saying anything, allowing her to continue.

"I heard Sonny say to his mom that she had to stop the stupidity. "We may not be rich, but we are decent, respected people," he said. "You should tell me who these people are and whatever you know about them, so I can help you and guide you properly." Gloria had shouted at him that she would not tell anything to anyone because then she would not get any money. Then I heard Sonny shouting that he would not come visit her again till she told him what was going on. He said he would wait for her phone call. I saw him walking in a huff to the front door. I ran back to the other side of the house to give the impression that I was just out for a walk. I saw Sonny driving away and I came back to my house."

Detective Tracer thanked Hannah for being so helpful. He took down her contact information and left. He was wondering why Sonny had deliberately chosen not to say anything about the matter. He decided it would be best to let the matter tarry until his next visit.

CHAPTER 5

At Château Pearson

It was Thursday morning and a beautiful day. Six days had elapsed since Gloria Solis's murder. The only suspect that police had was Dr. Ernest Pearson. Detective Tracer had taken up Gloria Solis's murder case on a priority basis and was going to question Dr. Ernest Pearson at his residence. He drove his yellow Volkswagen through the massive iron gates of Château Pearson and up the undulating private driveway surrounded by exquisitely manicured

lawns. The driveway was screened on
both sides by tall trees and ornamental
hedges. The beautiful but short drive led
to the spectacular manor house standing
majestically on over two acres of scenic land.

Everybody in Mayhaven knew that Dr.
Pearson was rich. The local news regularly
carried reports about him. At age forty-five, he
was still regarded as the most eligible bachelor
in town. Dr. Pearson had graduated from
Boston University and had gone to Princeton,
where he had obtained a doctorate in sociology.

Dr. Ernest Pearson's father was a
millionaire, but the two had never gotten
along smoothly. The senior Pearson owned
a flourishing horse farm. He had spent his
life raising, training and selling racehorses.
Regularly competing in major racing events
in the United States and Europe, his horses

often emerged winners. His son, however, had no interest in horses or horse racing. After completing his education, the junior Pearson had pursued a brilliant career in academics and had held a number of prestigious positions in reputed universities and other institutions of higher learning. His passions were history and archeology, areas in which he possessed a wealth of knowledge and expertise. He had authored and edited a number of books on antique art and led numerous archeological investigations. He had also studied in detail the customs and rituals of the aborigines of the Amazon. Some believed that he was obsessed with the subject of ancient history.

The elder Pearson had died some ten years ago. After his father's death, Dr. Ernest Pearson had inherited his father's entire estate. Although he never saw eye to eye with his father on many issues, and had preferred to stay away from him most of his adult life, after his death, he found he missed the old man terribly. He felt compelled to move back and settle in Mayhaven. He tried to manage his father's horse farm but failed repeatedly. He lacked the enthusiasm and talent required to work with thoroughbred horses. So, within one year of moving to Mayhaven, he had disposed off the horse farm and equipment. He then took up a position with Mayhaven's World Discovery Museum as its director and curator.

Dr. Pearson found the museum in complete disarray due to inadequate resources and mediocre planning and development. Years of neglect had resulted in decreased interest and dwindling attendance at the museum.

Dr. Ernest Pearson brought to the museum not only his much-needed expertise and passion, but he also lent funds from his own personal resources to make improvements. The results of his efforts were apparent. Under his zealous leadership, the museum flourished. He upgraded and enlarged the existing displays, diversified the exhibits and added new sections to keep in step with the changing times and needs.

Dr. Pearson had also initiated short-term period exhibitions of objects taken on loan from other museums and galleries. Some of the recent noteworthy exhibitions held recently were displays of rare reptilian specimens of the Amazon and collections of tribal masks from Asia, Africa and Europe, as well as the currently going kite exhibition. Naturally, the museum had started attracting visitors in droves.

Detective Edward Tracer parked his

car at the end of the driveway, next to a
red pickup truck. He got out and looked
around, struck by the captivating beauty of
the surroundings. There was the imposing
structure of the manor in the foreground
and a vibrant mountain range in the back.

He climbed the steps to a porch clad
in Italian marble and rang the bell. A tall,
angular, silver-haired housekeeper, wearing a
crisp green and yellow striped apron, answered
the door. Detective Tracer read her name on
her badge: Abigail. He introduced himself and
told her that he had come to see Dr. Pearson.

"Good morning, sir," Abigail responded.
"I will let Dr. Pearson know that you are
here. You may wait in the living room."

She led the detective into an almost
sky-high foyer with a grandiose crystal glass
chandelier hanging in the middle. One side

of the foyer led to an office with a majestic
library containing a highly ornate fireplace
and rich wood paneling. On the other side,
the foyer led to an exquisite living room with
designer furnishings and plate glass walls
providing a gorgeous view of the lush green
grounds through which he had just driven.

Edward walked into the living room,
taking in its splendor. The walls were adorned
with works of famous contemporary and
classical artists. Detective Tracer admired
the sweeping pinnacle view that unfolded
itself through the plate glass widows of the
living room. He saw his car parked next to
the red pickup truck on the driveway. A tall,
thin, dark man emerged from the side door
of the house. He was wearing baggy dark-
colored pants, a red-checkered shirt and
a black baseball cap, which he had pulled

down onto his forehead. Although the cap concealed the man's face, Edward noticed that the man had a beard. The man got into the red truck and drove down the driveway.

Edward walked closer to the window and watched the departing truck with rapt attention. He did not hear Dr. Pearson enter the room. He was therefore startled when Dr. Pearson greeted him in a crisp voice. "Good morning, Detective. What can I do for you today?"

"Good morning, Dr. Pearson," said Edward, turning to find Dr. Pearson standing right behind him. Edward told him that he had come to make a few routine inquiries regarding Dr. Pearson's lost gun and Gloria's murder.

Dr. Ernest Pearson pointed to the sofa and invited the detective to take a seat. He himself settled comfortably into

a matching leather chair placed opposite
the sofa.   Detective Tracer sat down
and took out his notebook. He wanted to
know if Dr. Pearson had any particular
reason to go to the bookstore that day
and personally talk with Gloria regarding
her work schedule at the museum.

"That morning I desperately needed
someone to come and clean the museum before
it opened to the public," explained Dr. Pearson.
"You see, the regular cleaning staff had
thoroughly vacuumed the place before they left
that night. Later that night, we had to move
a few things around to make space for a few
more entries that had arrived just at the very
last moment.The boxes containing the exhibits
had been delivered late, and it took us quite
some time to unload and stock them. Joseph,
who happens to be my housekeeper and

security guard at the museum, had promised to get the place tidy up before the museum opened at ten thirty the next morning. But Joseph suddenly took ill, and I was in a quandary about what to do. Gloria worked for the museum, but that was her day off. I hurried to the bookstore to catch her before she had finished her chores there and left."

"Where is Joseph now?" Asked Detective Tracer, writing down everything that Dr. Pearson was saying.

"I don't know," said Dr. Pearson in a low voice before looking away. "Joseph lives in the small guesthouse on my property. It is very convenient for both of us to have him living on the premises. He not only works at the museum, but he is also very helpful around the house and the gardens. However, I have not seen him since that day. He left suddenly last Friday and did not provide any contact address. For some time now, he has been mentioning that he might be going away for a few months. It was perhaps my mistake that I did not take him seriously." Dr. Pearson paused, uneasily looking out of the window.

Detective Edward immediately sensed that something was wrong. He peered in the direction where Ernest was looking and saw that the red truck was leaving again. It must have returned when he was talking to Dr. Pearson and his back was to the window.

"I think my going to the bookstore was prompted by a sort of mechanical reflex action," continued Dr. Pearson defensively. "Normally, I would have called the agency and asked them for help. But I was in a state of anxiety and wanted the job done in time. Gloria was my regular worker and could be trusted to do as told."

Detective Tracer looked at Dr. Ernest Pearson thoughtfully. He was trying hard to listen objectively and not come to any hasty comclusions. Still, he was finding it difficult to believe that Dr. Ernest Pearson, the director of Mayhaven's prestigious museum, would go to a bookstore looking for cleaning help. "Dr. Pearson, do you own a red truck?" He asked.

"No," said Dr. Pearson, "that red truck belongs to the gardener. Sometimes he loans it to Joseph."

Edward nodded as he wrote down that piece of information. "I also want to get details about your gun that has been missing. That very gun is apparently the weapon used in the killing. The police are looking for it. It is strange that the gun you reported missing two weeks ago should

turn out to be the weapon used to shoot
someone who works for you. Your presence
at the crime scene right about the time it
was committed is another complication.
Dr. Pearson, I won't mince words with you.
Your situation doesn't look good. Unless you
have a credible explanation, the needle of
suspicion is squarely pointing towards you."

The detective spoke slowly, watching
Dr. Pearson's face closely. "It can be argued
that Gloria came to know something that
could ruin you completely, and there was no
option but for you to silence her for good."

Dr. Pearson was turning perceptibly
pale. He put his finger to his nose, trying to
give an impression that either he was listening
very carefully or attempting to hide his
emotions. In fact, it was the latter, as his face
was beginning to twitch noticeably. That was

a clear indication that Dr. Pearson was finding it difficult to keep his emotions under control.

Dr. Pearson was finally able to put on a brave face. "Are you implying that I have something to do with the murder?" he asked curtly. "Well! If you have finished with your inquiry and have nothing more to do, you may leave. I have to get back to to my affairs."

Detective Tracer stared hard at Dr. Pearson, wondering why he should get so incensed. "Is there anything more you can tell me that can help us resolve this tangle?" he asked. "Otherwise, I would like to question Abigail regarding your lost gun and Joseph's whereabouts."

Dr. Pearson clearly did not like that idea and said stiffly, "Abigail has a lot of work to do. You can question her later when she is free."

Detective Edward gave a short grin

and said, "Dr. Pearson, I need to question Abigail now. Would you prefer that I get warrants for obstruction of justice?"

"No, no," responded Dr. Pearson. "I wouldn't stand in the path of justice. I was only thinking about Abigail being free from her chores first. Now that you insist let us find her, and you can question her."

Dr. Pearson led Detective Tracer through the formal dining room. The room had eye-catching murals on one wall and etched glass windows on the other. Ernest was not only very rich, but he also had refined taste, thought Edward, soaking in the grandeur of the place.

They walked through the dining room to the spacious kitchen, where Abigail and a man were eating breakfast. Edward noticed that Abigail and her friend were very surprised to see Dr. Pearson walking into kitchen with Detective Tracer following him.

"Hey, Dan," said Dr. Pearson. "Good morning. I didn't know you are here early."

Detective Tracer looked at both the men. To him it seemed that Dr. Pearson was fully aware that Dan came in early every morning to have breakfast with Abigail.

"Good Morning. Dr. Pearson. You know, I try to start early, but today it is really not all that early," said Dan Wall sheepishly. "It is eight thirty already."

"Good morning sir. I was waiting for your instructions to bring some refreshments for your guest," said Abigail.

Dr. Pearson winked at Abigail. "Gail, the detective would like to ask you a few questions." He then invited Detective Tracer to go ahead with the questioning.

"I would like to talk to her alone. Can we

go to the library," he inquired of Dr. Pearson.

"Sure, please feel at home," said
Dr. Pearson. He instructed Abigail to take
Detective Tracer to the library and also see
him off after they had finished talking because
he was leaving shortly for the museum.

Dr. Pearson turned to the detective,
held out his hand and said graciously,
"Good meeting you and best of luck to you
to solve this puzzle. Let me know if I can be
of any further assistance in the matter."

Detective Tracer shook
Dr. Pearson's extended hand and
thanked him for his cooperation.

Abigail led Detective Tracer back
through the dining room and the living
room. Once in the library, she gave her
statement, confirming that Dr. Pearson
was home at the time of the murder.

"Dr. Pearson left home around seven thirty that morning," she said with certainty. "I took his tea and newspaper upstairs at seven, as his usual routine is to have his tea while reading the daily paper. Then he typically exercises while watching the news on TV. Afterwards, he showers, dresses and comes down for breakfast at nine. That day, there was a phone call from Joseph at seven thirty. I do not know what was said but Dr. Pearson left home in a hurry. He looked greatly upset."

"How about the gun? Do you know anything about the lost gun?"

Abigail said that she had not known that Dr. Pearson owned a gun until he reported it missing to the police. "Police came here last week for an investigation. They made a thorough search but nothing was found."

Abigail suddenly became emotional

and started crying. "I miss Gloria. We went
to the same church. Sometimes, if Maria
our regular help could not come, then Gloria
would come here to clean. She would sit in
the kitchen, at the table near window and
eat her lunch. She always brought her own
food. She did not care about the leftovers
that I offered her on few occassions. She
was very quiet and never talked about
herself but she had a kind heart.She once
gave me a statue of Saint Francis. She had
a firm faith in the powers of Saint Francis,
a patron saint of the animal kingdom. "

"About two or three weeks ago, I heard
her being cross with Dr. Pearson. It was
strange. She was saying that he was cheap,
and that he would not get away with it. It had
something to do with Saint Francis. I heard
her say that the idol of the saint belongs to

the church—not to a box. She said he would come to grief. Gloria wanted Dr. Pearson to return something to Mexico or she would go to the police. Joseph knows more about the argument than me because he was listening at the library door. He was very upset too. I do not like Joseph. He has been with the Pearson family for twenty-five years, and it's gone to his head. He now thinks and behaves as if he is one of them, sometimes acting as if he knows what is best for Dr. Pearson."

"Where is Joseph now?" asked Detective Tracer.

"I do not know," she pursed her lips and was quiet for a minute before adding, "I have not seen him at the house or working in the garden for the last week. He has not been in the tool shed either. He has a hobby of woodworking so he spends lot of his spare time in that place, which is good because

I do not like him hanging around in the

kitchen. I just cannot stand his swaggering

about. I am sure you know what I mean."

Detective Tracer felt that Abigail

was telling the truth. Although he was

wondering why Dr. Pearson had not told him

about the argument with Gloria, he did not

want to distress Abigail any further, so he

prepared to leave. Before saying goodbye,

he gave his card to her and said, "Abigail,

if you remember something or need help

you can reach me at this number."

Abigail led the detective out of the

library to the foyer. Outside, Edward again

stopped to admire the breathtaking view. On

one side of the house, a beautifully manicured

lawn sloped gently into a wild woodland

garden where brightly colored daisies and

wildflowers provided a captivating ground cover. Variety of trees lent elegance to the colorful walkway into the woodlands.

On the other side of the house were beautiful formal gardens. There were trees with pink and white flowers and tall trees with clouds of lavender flowers touching the sky. Tiny flowers in a myraid of colors were springing up everywhere. What a wonderful place to live, thought Edward as he got in his car and drove back to the station.

CHAPTER 6

An Unclaimed Key Ring

It was Friday once again. Exactly a week had elapsed since Gloria's murder. Boris was opening his store for the first time since that fateful day and was still struggling to reconcile with Gloria's gruesome death in his store. Police had turned his store upside down looking for clues. Lying near the body, they had found a key ring containing only one key.

The police had placed the time of murder roughly between six thirty and eight thirty in the morning, but it was probably closer to seven o' clock, because Gloria had finished vacuuming, made coffee and picked up the newspapers. However, she had not yet started dusting the shelves. It was clear that the murder was committed by an acquaintance of Gloria because the store door was unlocked and there were no signs of any struggle or robbery.

Boris had spent the weekend at his mother's house. She owned a rustic little cottage close to the beach. It was a two-hour drive from Mayhaven. Boris was about ten years old when they migrated to the States from Russia. His mom knew very little English at the time but upon arrival in the United States, she had taken classes and had become fluent in the language. For fifteen years, she was employed with the local library in Mayhaven as a librarian for the children's section. Because his mother could not afford to send him to day care, Boris had spent almost all his young life, including after-school hours, weekends, summer and winter breaks, at the library. He had grown up with books and had read a lot during his formative years. Naturally, with his inherent affinity for books, he ended up running a bookstore. He still loved to read.

Gloria's murder in his bookstore had him worried. His mother was now very concerned about his safety and had strongly urged him never to let his guard down while he was in the store. She made Boris promise that he would be careful. When Boris left his mother that morning, she had given him a bagful of homemade petrozkis—a delicious Russian snack.

Boris was apprehensive when he opened the store. He thought the store would be a

mess since its last opening a week earlier.
However, he was surprised to find that most
of the things were in their place. There was a
chalk diagram of the corpse, where Gloria's
body had been found. Boris got busy cleaning
the store, first removing the chalk mark from
the floor. He was worried about the negative
effect of the murder on the reputation of
his store. He was therefore contemplating
giving the store a face lift by refreshing the
displays on the shelves and adding new
touches to the décor in the windows to make
things look different and cheerful. The store
already smelt better because aroma of fresh
coffee was beginning to fill the air. Boris
had made coffee as soon as he came in.

Ding-dong! Went the bell. Boris got up
from the floor where he was cleaning the chalk
marks and walked to the front of the store.

"Good morning!" came a cheerful greeting from the door. "Is the store open?" Boris was taken by surprise and was mighty pleased to see Dr. Darshan Singh and his wife entering the store. Anu was looking striking in a green Punjabi salwar kameez outfit, comprised of baggy trousers and a knee-length shirt, popular in the northern parts of India.

"Good morning," he said. "What brings you here so early? He shared an extremely cordial relationship with the Singh family. "Your mom informed me that you would be opening the store today, so we decided to drop by to extend our best wishes," said Anu. Not only was Anu a friend of Boris's mother, but she was a frequent visitor to the store as well. She purchased all the school supplies, stationery items, books, music and so forth from Kanega Books and Music.

"Thank you," said Boris. He told them the details of the previous Friday morning. "Police have very few suspects and are not anywhere close to solving the murder."

"There is something very unnatural about Dr. Pearson coming to the store to talk to Gloria," noted Darshan. "Why would he arrive so early that morning? Was it normal for Dr. Pearson to come here to talk to her? He could have telephoned her at home later in the day."

"Well, I was surprised to see him too. He looked unduly anxious and worried. I don't recall seeing him ever coming here to talk to Gloria. I wonder if he was used to coming to the store prior to my arrival. Anyway, I think I will be able to open the store today. Please have some coffee and petrozkis."

Darshan and Anu helped themselves to coffee and the inviting petrozkis.

Anu added her thoughts. "I keep wondering why Dr. Pearson was at the store so early. He does not look like a murderer, but who knows. This does not seem like a random murder. The motive is highly perplexing. There was no robbery of any type. Maybe Dr. Pearson killed Gloria and was still in the store when you came in, and then pretended to come from outside. I am convinced that Dr. Pearson is not entirely innocent. He has something to do with this."

"Dr. Ernest Pearson was not in the store when I came in. It is not possible. He had indeed come from outside. You see, he was soaking wet from the rain when I saw him. The rain didn't start until after I got in the store. If he was already in the store and had opened the door from inside, he could not be soaking wet." Boris started to replace the newspapers in the newspaper stand.

Anu and Darshan walked around
to the CD section. "When did you get the
cameras installed?" Inquired Darshan.

"I got them recently. I was losing a lot of
music CDs to the shoplifters. People generally
love to hang around in the CD section, and
some of them, when they realize no one is
watching, tend to pocket and walk away
with a CD or two. Placing the cameras here
will surely deter shoplifters. Unfortunately, I
wasn't leaving the cameras routinely running
all the time. I'd turn them on in the morning
and switch them off at closing time. Now I
will be leaving the cameras on all the time."

"Did the police find
anything?" asked Darshan.

"Near the body, under the card shelf,
they found a key ring with a single key. I was

still here when they found it. The key ring
has a wooden carved skull sculpture like
an animal face or something. They asked
me if it belonged to me. It didn't. Maybe it
was Gloria's or belonged to a customer or
the killer left it. We don't know yet. Police
did not think it had much relevance. I
still have it in my lost and found safe."

Boris showed them the key on a key ring.
The miniature wooden mask like sculpture
with pearl like seashells for eyes on the key
ring looked very quaint. "It appears to be hand
made. I wonder who made it?" Remarked
Anu as she carefully inspected the key ring.

As Boris put the key away, he said,
"Gloria was very happy during the last few
weeks. She was planning to return to Mexico
and visit her friends and relatives. She was
even thinking of going back permanently. She

said that she would have enough money to retire and settle in Mexico. She was sure she would not have to work ever again. This was very surprising to me. All her life, her meager income barely covered her daily expenses. How could she suddenly have such a big windfall?"

"Boris," said Darshan, "did you see anything unusual that day? Maybe someone running in the street?"

"Nothing unusual. Even the garbage truck was at the usual spot, near the coffee shop, as it is every Friday morning.

"Oh yes," said Anu. "The garbage truck is right there today also—on Friday at eight twenty. We came early because we wanted to catch you before you opened the store and got busy with your customers." She deliberately walked to the door and looked at the garbage truck, that was slowly turning onto the next street. "Maybe the garbage truck driver saw something."

"Do you know if the police questioned the driver of the garbage truck?" Darshan asked Boris.

"I'm not sure."

"Well, we should be going," said Darshan. "We have to take the kids to see the museum."

"Thank you very much for the coffee and petrozkis," said Anu.

"All the best and take care of yourself," said Darshan. "I am sure the police will catch the murderer very soon."

Darshan and Anu walked to their car, which was parked on the next street, the same street onto which the garbage truck had turned.

"Hey, Doc!" called Mark, the

garbage truck driver. "How are you?"

Darshan turned to see Mark waving from the truck's window. He was a tall, burly man and always had a baseball hat backwards on his head.

"Hello Mark," said Darshan. "How is your son? Did his fever go down?" Mark had brought his son to Darshan's clinic with a high fever a few days earlier.

"He is doing good," said Mark as he jumped out of the truck to talk to the Singhs.

"What are you doing here so early?"

"We came to see Boris and extend him our greetings, as he is opening his store after a lapse of some time," said Anu. "It was so sad that Gloria had such a grisly end. I cannot believe that a week has already gone by. How the time flies."

"Oh yes. It was so weird. I was

right here when the blare of police sirens startled me. This place was literally crawling with police cars last Friday."

"Did you see anything suspicious?" asked Anu.

"Well, everything was different last week, what with the thunderstorm. People were running down the street, hurrying to take cover, and the police cars were overcrowding the place. Even Joseph Slayer, who works at the museum and who is the housekeeper at the Pearson residence, was running down the street with a coat pulled over his face. I called to him, but he didn't respond, or perhaps he didn't hear me. Well, I cannot blame him. Everyone was scurrying to get where they had to go because of the rain.

"Anyway, I should be going," said Mark. "I just wanted to thank you for your help at the clinic. Have a good day." He jumped back into the truck. He whistled as he started his truck and waved goodbye to the Singhs as he drove the truck slowly and carefully down the road.

"So, Ernest and Joseph were both here on Friday," said Anu. "Wait till I give this information to Detective Tracer on Monday. I think this murder has something to do with Mayhaven's World Discovery Museum."

"Here we go. Detective Anu is on to something," teased Darshan. "I think volunteering at the police station is having an effect on you. You are now beginning to see clues and evidence everywhere. It's time you moved on to other hobbies such as bake sales."

They were laughing as they got into the car to drive back home.

CHAPTER 7

Sleuths at the Museum

Anu and Darshan returned home to find Shawn and Jasmine already dressed for the visit to the museum. Jasmine and Holly were playing on Aker's driveway, making drawings with chalk, while Steven, Holly's father, was working in the yard nearby. Shawn and Jordan were in Shawn's house, playing "Divsion of Honor" on computer.

"Daddy, when are we leaving for the Museum?" asked Jasmine, looking sprightly in her denim Bermuda shorts, a striped polo shirt and striped slides. She was holding a straw basket bag, which contained her digital camera, an extra memory card and batteries for the camera.

"You look ready to go. We plan to leave in about an hour. Is that okay, Anu?" Darshan asked his wife.

"That's fine. I can toss up an early lunch before we leave." She prepared a lunch of pasta, salad and Southern fried chicken. Everyone was hungry and the food soon disappeared. Darshan helped Anu clean up after lunch.

The doorbell rang as Anu was putting away the last dish.

"I'll get it," said Jasmine, running to the door. "It's probably Holly."

"Hi, Jasmine!" said Holly. "You look very pretty."

"You look very nice too," replied Jasmine. Holly was wearing capris with a red ribbon belt, a yellow cotton polo shirt, flower wedge sandals and a striped twill wristlet.

"We're leaving soon," said Jasmine. She and Holly walked outside, talking excitedly.

Shawn came running down the stairs. "Hey, Jordan! I see you have a cell phone. Is it yours?"

"No, it's my mom's," said Jordan. "She let me borrow it just for today. Next year I'll get my own cell phone and also get my driver's permit."

"Me too," said Shawn. "I cannot wait to get behind the wheel of my very own Corvette." They were laughing as they joined Holly and Jasmine on the driveway, waiting for Jasmine and Shawn's parents.

A few moments later, they were

climbing into Dr. Singh's seven-seat family van to drive to the museum to see the 'Kites From Around The World' exhibition. As they approached the museum, they were surprised by the large number of buntings and streamers that had been put across the street to extend a cheerful welcome to visitors.

"Dr. Pearson has worked hard to improve the museum's profile," said Anu smiling. "It used to be a small museum focusing only on local history. No one even knew that it existed."

"The first time we visited the museum was about four years ago when my school brought us here for a field trip," said Shawn. "An exhibition of rare coins was on display at that time."

"Remember that big hoopla that erupted seven or eight years ago when the authorities were proposing to shut down the museum?" said Darshan. "Dr. Pearson had just taken over as its director a couple of years earlier. It was mainly the result of his strenuous efforts that the motion to close the place for good was defeated. Since then Dr. Pearson has been working hard to upgrade the image of the place and diversify its activities. His first initiative was to enter into successful collaboration arrangements with fellow art galleries, museums and display centers. He periodically began to organize high-profile subject-oriented exhibitions to bring exotic objects from around the world, things nobody ever got to see previously."

"Currently, the museum holds a variety of permanent collections of classical paintings, period costumes, curios and relics excavated from historical sites, statues and similar art wares, wax figures and native American arts," said Anu as Darshan parked the car in the museum's parking lot. "Dr. Pearson himself has donated his own collection of paintings, which are also on display in the museum. Despite its limited size, the museum has steadily come to acquire an enviable regional reputation." The group alighted from the car and walked up to the gate to purchase the entry tickets.

Mayhaven's World Discovery Museum was housed in a two storey house built in the early 1800s and surrounded by lush green gardens. The ten-bedroom house had belonged to Mr. Mayhaven, the first mayor of the city. The house was built on a lot of over seven acres. The original architectural features of the building had been preserved carefully to retain its aura of antiquity.

At the entrance gate, a young woman

dressed in an eighteenth-century costume
greeted the visitors. The costume was called
a day dress and comprised of a long skirt
with hoops under the skirt. She was talking
to a group of four people and invited the
Singh family to join the group. She then led
the group for a guided tour of the museum.

Inside the museum, time seemed to have
stood still. The first floor of the building housed
a wax museum displaying wax figures in
eighteenth-century costumes in all the rooms.
One room on the floor was made up in the
manner of a bedroom in the home of an upper-
class family of the time. It was furnished with
a four-poster bed, two chairs, a dresser and an
armoire, all made of top-grade mahogany wood.

The living room on the first floor
overflowed with a medley of vintage
heirlooms and prized curios, some of them

dating over two centuries ago. There was
a grand piano, an elaborate wooden settee
with inlaid Masonic symbols, an ornately
painted wooden tourist chest from Mexico,
a collection of old records played on a pump
organ, a gramophone and a Spanish revival
iron chandelier. There was a beautiful chest
tucked in a corner. It was made of sandalwood
and was full of toys. The toys had belonged
to an eighteenth-century princely family
of Mysore in India. The walls of the living
room carried paintings done by old masters
including Van Gogh and Leonardo da Vinci.
It was not known from where the museum
had procured all these invaluable exhibits.

"I like that chest with sweet
smelling wooden toys," said Holly.

The group walked into the dining
room, which had a stately mahogany dining

table in the centre. The dining room walls also had exquisite paintings by reputed masters. "The dining table, as well as its crockery and cutlery, were also from the eighteenth century, once belonging to a royal household," said Jordan, reading from the accompanying plaque.

The dining room led into the kitchen, which was also furnished with gadgets from the eighteenth century. Particularly eye catching were the old-style cooking oven and stove. Also on display in a corner were an old model sewing machine, a radio set and an ancient model telephone instruments with separate ear and mouthpieces. Jasmine was taking pictures for her scrapbook. A few other groups of visitors were also taking pictures.

Shawn and Jordan were looking carefully at the wax figures in all the rooms.

The figures were dressed in clothes popularly worn in the eighteenth century. The clothes covered every inch of the body of the wax figures except their hands and feet.

"I wonder how they felt during the summer," said Shawn.

"Well, in those days, people wore the same clothes year-round," said the guide . "It was considered indiscreet for a woman to go in public without being robed in a proper full dress. The skirts in those days were more or less ankle long. Even up until a century or so ago, it was reported that upper-class households in England even clothed the legs of tables and chairs."

"Schools organize the field trips to the museum so children can see firsthand the way life used to be in those days," said Anu.

Darshan chuckled. "Yes, maybe

the hand-operated sewing machines are
antiquated here in the States, but they are still
in use in homes and tailoring shops in India.
Therefore, if one wants to get a live view of how
life moved in the preceding century, a visit to
India would be more revealing than a visit to
the museum." Darshan and Anu always grew
nostalgic when they saw housewares such as
a manual old-style sewing machine and bulky
box radio on display as antiques because back
home in India these artices were cherished
a lot as family heirlooms and the sewing
machines were still in use a lot by their moms.

The group slowly climbed the winding
stairway to the second floor, which had
two hall-sized rooms on the left side.
One of the rooms displayed paintings
from Dr. Pearson's private collection.
The second room was currently in use

as the venue for the kite exhibition.

The right side had two similar rooms. The first was the antiquity room, which housed the recently acquired objet d' art, including paintings, sculptures, statuary, carvings and other effects. Additionally, the room had on display a popular collection of masks procured by Dr. Pearson from a museum in Russia for an undisclosed sum. The collection had an extensive range of masks in popular use in all parts of the world, both in ancient and modern times.

The other room was the costume room, which also had two sections—ancient and modern. The costumes had been acquired from all over the world. A visit to the costume room was highly popular with children because of the novel diversion introduced again by Dr. Pearson. Every child visiting this section was shown a variety of costumes worn by different characters, including drummers, hunters, villagers, milkmaids, princesses, monks, etc. The child was given an option to select any particular costume. A replica of the selected costume was then lent to the child, who tried it on and play acted the role of the character associated with that costume.

"If a child picked out the costume worn by a drummer," said Anu, "he would have to act like a drummer."

"Wow, that sounds like fun," said Darshan.

"Come on, Dad, why don't you select and try on a dress!" Exclaimed Shawn in jest.

"Oh, no. I'm not a child anymore. Also, we are short of time. We still have to cover the mask room. It's something new. One of my colleagues brought her

son here the other day and was full of
praise for the entries on display."

Shawn had visited the museum with
his school four years ago. Since then the
museum had grown at a rapid pace. The layout
plan of the gardens around the museum had
been completely modified to impart an added
flavour of antiquity. There were also such
new additions as a kitchen garden, an herb
garden and an orange grove. The piece de
resistance of the place was a romantic garden
which had statues of selected Shakespearean
characters installed in different nooks.

"Joseph, Dr. Pearson's devoted
housekeeper, also supervises the
upkeep of the gardens, apart from his
regular multi-fold household duties and
involvements," said Anu. "After we have
finished going through the interiors, we

should also take a tour of the gardens."

A year earlier, Dr. Pearson had put up a spacious storage room at the back of the gardens. The storage room had huge gates that remained closed most of the time. The popular expectation at the time was that he might be planning to add another section to the museum, but things had remained at a standstill.

"Another room has been added to the basement," noted Anu. "It will serve as an activity room for educational purposes for the children."

Dr. Pearson's office was at the end of the hall, next to the costume room. As the group passed the office to enter the costume room, Shawn, out of curiosity, tried to peek inside the office through the slightly ajar door. However, the file cabinets placed near the entrance door blocked his view. Shawn saw his group follow the guide into the costume room. He was alone in the hallway and out of curiosity decided to enter and take a quick peek.

Shawn slipped inside. The room was empty. Dr. Pearson's desk was in the center of the room and cluttered hopelessly. "Looks like Dr. Pearson is a busy man," thought Shawn. He looked around and came upon a crumpled piece of paper in the wastepaper basket. Acting on an impulse, he pocketed the paper immediately. There was also a fax machine in the room. The red light on the machine was blinking, signaling that the machine had run out of paper. Shawn automatically loaded paper into the machine. His father had shown him how to do that. A fax message was received. Shawn picked it up and read it: "Pickup Saturday night at 10:30 p.m."

Shawn heard voices from the doorway. He could not see anyone, nor could anyone see him because of the file cabinets. Shawn stuffed the fax message into his pocket and dashed out of the room through the other door. He found himself in the costume room. He stood for a minute near the door and listened to the conversation.

He heard one soft-cultured voice say, "Fax should be here by now, and it's not. Highly surprising. The machine is on, and the paper tray is loaded."

Then Shawn heard a gruff, heavily accented voice say, "Well, give me the phone number."

"Oh! The phone number. I threw it in the wastepaper basket, which is now empty and lying toppled on its side," said the cultured voice of Dr. Pearson. "Looks like someone was here. When I came to my office earlier in the morning, I saw that the fax machine was empty, but I didn't have time to load paper. And now not only there is paper in the machine but the paper with the phone number is gone as well."

Shawn heard a sound almost like an angry growl which he presumed was from the owner of the heavily accented gruff voice. Then he heard footsteps coming towards the door where he was standing. Terrified, Shawn moved away from the door.

CHAPTER 8

An Unpleasant Encounter

There was a group of visitors assembled in the middle of the room, gathered around a slim girl dressed in an eighteenth-century costume. Shawn sought refuge in numbers and mingled with the group. The girl was giving live demonstrations of the uses for an array of ancient household gadgets, such as a sewing machine, a spinning wheel and a charcoal-fired iron.

Shawn glanced towards the door from where he had just emerged. He spied two men rushing through it and then coming to a halt. One was a tall, dark, mean-looking bald man with a scar on his right cheek. He was wearing a black leather jacket and motorcycle boots. The other was a well-dressed, bespectacled, medium-height man with thin gray hair, a broad fleshy face, a thin pointed nose and small eyes. The well-dressed man was holding a red book in his hand.

Spotting his mom, Shawn waved to her. Anu waved back and glanced at the door behind Shawn. The two men were still standing there. Anu recognized one of the men as Dr. Pearson. She had met him once when she had chaperoned the class trip from Shawn's school to the museum.

"That's Dr. Pearson," she whispered to Darshan and started walking in the direction of the two men. Darshan followed

her. They both smiled at Dr. Ernest
Pearson and greeted him warmly.

"Hello, Dr. Pearson," said
Darshan. "How are you doing?"

"Hello, Dr. Singh," smiled Dr. Pearson
as he greeted Anu and darshan. He shook
hands with Dr. Singh and his wife.

"I hope you are enjoying your visit here."

"Yes, of course," said Darshan.
"Your displays and shows are
certainly pulling in large crowds."

"Thank you for your kind words, but
frankly we were expecting an even bigger
gathering. Please enjoy yourselves."

"I saw a lot of boxes in the back," Anu
said to Dr. Pearson. "Are you planning further
additions to the museum and its activities?
You have got a lot going on for the museum,
what with adding new wings to the building

and organizing such innovative exhibitions."

Dr. Pearson nodded but did
not reply. Instead, he glanced at the
man standing next to him. Anu also
glanced at the intimidating man.

"By the way," Dr. Pearson said to
the tall man with him, "this is Dr. Singh
and his wife, Anu. Dr. Singh runs the
only emergency clinic in Mayhaven. So
if you were to fall sick here, you would
have no choice but to go to his clinic."

He turned to Darshan and Anu and said,
"Meet my new associate, Karl Sorley. Karl is
from Czechoslovakia and is here to help us
remodel the museum. You are correct in that
we are planning to add a few more sections.
I have just obtained the needed approval
from the authorities and am now on a hunt
for a competent architect who can make the

needed changes while preserving the original design of the building. We are contemplating a kind of remodeling and readjustment exercise only. The idea is to make the maximum use of the available space."

"Hello, Mr. Sorley," said Dr. Singh and his wife together. Karl simply gave a cold nod.

"It was a shock to learn about the death of Gloria," said Anu to Ernest. "Such a poor unassuming woman. And such a tragic end."

"Yes, indeed," responded Dr. Pearson slowly. "It is truly sad. But life has to move on." Dr. Ernest Pearson seemed uncomfortable about the turn the conversation was taking. He hurriedly excused himself and started to hail another group of visitors.

Karl glowered at Dr. Singh and his wife Anu and said in a European accent, "Be Kareful, Daktor! It is always good to mind your own beezness. Too much prying is never been good for anyone."

Anu and Darshan were taken aback by what sounded like a threat. Anu could not help thinking that Sorley should be spelled Sourly.

Dr. Pearson had heard Karl's threatening words to the Singh family. He turned around from the couple that he had just started talking to, signaling Karl to be quiet. He started to apologize to the Singhs, but before he could complete his sentence, there was a loud command from Jasmine.

"Smile!" she said. Instinctively, everyone turned to her as there was a blinding flash. Jasmine was quick to click a group photo of her parents with Dr. Pearson and Karl.

"Hey, no pictures!" shouted Karl. Jasmine shrank back timidly.

Anu stepped between Karl and Jasmine,

her eyes glaring into his. "Why are you scaring her? She's only a little girl taking pictures for her scrapbook. It's her hobby."

Dr. Pearson paled visibly and apologized for his associate's behavior. He told Karl to go back in the office. He placated Jasmine, telling her not to mind Karl's behavior. She should feel free to take as many pictures as she wanted to.

Anu put an arm around Jasmine and told her to keep moving with the group. She looked around for Shawn, who was at the window with Holly and Jordan, admiring the view. Jasmine too joined the group and took pictures of the view.

The group then slowly moved towards the mask room, which had more than two hundred masks on display. The door of the mask room displayed a crocodile mask on each panel. The masks were made from wood and painted in traditional African tribal designs.

"The dancers wear these masks during their ceremonial performances of the crocodile dance," said the guide. "The dancers usually cavort in pairs with fluid undulating motions." Then the guide pointed to the top of the doors, which featured famous swooping hawk mask. The guide called the group's attention to the checkerboard design feature of both the Swooping Hawk mask and the Crocodile masks. "This pattern signifies a complex mélange of knowledge and ignorance," he informed his attentive group. Meanwhile the members of the group were oohing and aahing as they took their time appreciating the masks and voicing their admiration as they entered the mask room. Just inside the room on the left wall was a leopard mask from Egypt. It too captured everyone's attention.

Anu, Darshan and the kids were at the tail end of the group. As they were entering the mask room, examining the masks displayed on the door and the walls, Anu was taken aback as she recognized one of the mask on the wall. "That mask looks like a full-size replica of the miniature wooden sculpture on the key ring Boris showed us this morning," she whispered to Darshan.

Darshan looked closely at the mask and agreed. "You're right. It looks like the same face, except the key ring sculpture did not have the same smooth, textured surface and so many details as this mask. Maybe that's due to the miniature size of the key ring figure."

"We should bring this to Detective Tracer's attention. I have suspected

throughtout that somehow Gloria's murder
was connected to this museum."

"You'll be seeing him on Monday,"
her husband said. "Let him know then."

The room was overflowing with
masks from every continent. The masks
were displayed category wise in different
sections. In each section, the masks were
further grouped into the regions from which
they had originated. Right at the entry point,
one was greeted by an array of bewitching
Yup'ik masks from Southwest Alaska.
The masks were originally used on formal
occasions for group dancing. They were
made of wood and decorated with beads and
feathers representing animals or spirits.

"There are masks made of
almost every material: clay, leather,
wood, feathers, seashells and even

seal hair," remarked Shawn.

"Shawn, let's go to the section displaying African masks," proposed Jordan.

Masks in the African section were categorized according to their uses. Awe inspiring helmet masks such as the Wabele masks used by the Poro tribe and the Pumbu masks used by Eastern Pende chiefs were displayed as icons of power.

The guide kept on talking as he led the group through different sections designated as icons of powers, images of ancestors and faces of spirits. "Masks had a special significance in tribal life in ancient times. They were an essential item of wear at ceremonial gatherings, including periodic celebrations of festivals.

"This mask here with the large eyes, ears and nose," elaborated the guide, "symbolizes the wise protector and healer, which, in other words, means an ancient African witch doctor."

The guide picked up another piece. "This is the mask of the tribal chief, depicting the insignia of the chief's nurturing and protective powers."

The masks from South and Central America were more human looking than those in the African collection. Particularly eye catching was 'La Borracha,' which literally means a drunken woman. The mask portrayed an oversized slatternly feminine face with unkempt hair, garishly painted lips and eyes oozing with mascara.

"I never thought that masks had such a long-going, high-flying heritage," said Anu as she saw Shawn, Jordan, Jasmine and Holly admiring the masks and reading the legends about each one. "This visit here has been such an educational and enlightening experience."

The next room hosted the highly advertised "Kites from Around the World" exhibition. There were colorful kites from different countries mounted upon walls and ceilings. Everyone was lost in their colorful splendor. The reds were so bright, the greens so pretty, the blues so soothing, the purples so royal and the yellows were like sunflowers blooming on a sunny day.

The other end of the room had shelves full of relics and antiques from various early civilizations from Asia, especially India and China. Everyone was finally satiated with the new information.

"It was an interesting day, Daddy," said Jasmine. "But all this reading and walking has made me tired and hungry."

"Well, I think they have ice cream in their cafeteria," said Darshan.

"Ice cream sounds really
good," said Shawn.

"I don't want ice cream," said Jordan.
"I would prefer something like a salad."

Everyone laughed, knowing Jordan
had recently become a health fiend.

"I want ice cream," said Holly.
"I need it for an energy boost."

They went through the hallway
and then downstairs to the cafeteria. Dr.
Darshan Singh let everyone order according
to his or her preference. Shawn ordered a
chocolate milkshake. Jasmine had a banana
boat sundae with one scoop of strawberry
icecream and a scoop of chocolate icecream.
Holly had vanilla ice cream sundae with
strawberry and cookies while Jordan had
a salad and lemonade. Darshan and Anu
ordered coffee with sugar and cream.

With their cameras, Jasmine and Holly had taken a bunch of pictures of kites, masks and views from the windows. They reviewed the pictures while eating their snacks.

Finally, Shawn and Jordan walked up to Dr. Singh and Anu, who were engrossed in the view of the gardens from the cafeteria patio. "We're ready to go home," announced Shawn. Jasmine and Holly were also eager to leave.

"Everyone seems to have had a good time," observed Dr. Singh as they all piled into the van for the drive back home.

"It's a small museum so we actually had time to look at everything," said Anu. "Did you notice that the permanent collection included only the furniture, appliances, paintings, costumes and the recently acquired assemblage of tribal masks?"

"Their permanent collection is not of

the same stature as the Getty Museum or other bigger museums, but Dr. Pearson has successfully made the museum popular by holding exhibitions of exotic objects that people would not get to see otherwise," said Dr. Singh.

It was only a fifteen-minute drive back and everyone was quiet on the way home. Anu reminded the kids that they had a Bhangra practice session the next day. Bhangra is a traditional Indian folk dance known for its robust movements and pulsating music.

CHAPTER 9

Tell Tale Photos

"Mom, what do you have for breakfast?" inquired a sleepy Jasmine as she came down the stairs.

Anu looked up from her newspaper. "Depends on what you'd like to eat."

Darshan and Shawn were playing Jenga, a game involving removal of blocks from a tower like stack of blocks without letting the tower topple over. This was the third time they had set up the stack. Darshan had won the first two games. The clear rationale behind

Darshan's two consecutive victories was his conservative approach. He seldom took any risks. On the other hand, Shawn was a risk taker by nature, always attempting the impossible and making the tower topple.

Once again, they started removing blocks from the stack. Only one piece was taken out each time and was then placed on the top of the tower, taking care not to tumble the stack. Some blocks became loose and were therefore easier to take out.

Shawn, with his usual airs of bravado, was pulling out difficult pieces. Darshan, with his usual patience, was cautiously removing only the loose blocks. Shawn urged his father to take a risk. "Dad! Try to take out a piece from the bottom. It's more fun."

"Shawn, I can see through you. I am your dad and I know what you're trying to do.

You are trying to tempt me to take a risk so I lose. But I would rather be safe than sorry."

"Dad, take a bottom piece," coaxed Shawn. "Come on, I challenge you."

Finally, Darshan took Shawn's challenge and tried to pull out one of the pieces on the bottom. The tower toppled and Shawn was ecstatic.

"I won!" he shouted in glee.

Jasmine looked at them and then settled comfortably on her daddy's lap. "I want pancakes," she announced.

"Okay then, pancakes for everyone?" questioned Anu. No one dissented, which meant the proposition was acceptable to everyone. Soon the Singh family room was filled with the appetizing aroma of fresh pancakes which made everyone realize how famished they were. Darshan got up and

squeezed fresh orange juice while Jasmine
set the table. Shawn hovered around glowing
because of his recent victory at having tricked
his father into pulling out a risky piece.

Finally, Darshan said to Shawn, "Shawn,
the most important thing in a game is to play.
It is immaterial whether you win or lose. The
important thing is to keep the game going.
Failures too can give you a lesson or two
to further hone and perfect your skills."

"Fine, Dad, but you have to admit I have
excellent persuasion skills. I made you pull
that piece out against your better judgment."

"Okay, you win," said Darshan. "Keep
it up! If you have good persuasion skills, you
can turn out to be a good salesperson."

"Thank you dad," said Shawn.
"I will take that as a compliment."

Darshan started helping Anu with

preparing eggs and Shawn ran upsatirs to start downloading pictures from Jasmine's digital camera. After he finished downloading the pictures, Shawn too joined the family at the table. During breakfast, Shawn narrated his personal experience at the museum and showed the two pieces of crumpled paper he had taken from Dr. Pearson's office. Dr. Singh examined the papers cursorily and then proceeded to reprimand Shawn for his indiscrete act. "Shawn, these papers are evidence that you have turned into a thief and cannot be trusted. What ever your reasons might be you cannot pick up someone else's property. Even law enforcement authorities have to procure a warrant before they can search any place."

"Sorry dad. I don't know what I was thinking when I pocketed the papers from Dr. Pearson's office."

Shawn started to pour thick maple syrup on his pancakes. Much to his mom's dismay, he covered every inch of the pancakes with syrup. He then proceeded to devour gleefully the drenched pancakes with a slurp, leaving a trail of syrup dripping from his chin to the table. Jasmine stared with rapt attention and then followed suit. Darshan and Anu watched them with silent amusement.

Dr. Singh picked up the crumpled pieces of papers that Shawn had given him and handed them to Anu saying, "I'm going to get ready. I have to be at the clinic within an hour."

Everyone else helped clean the breakfast table.

Jasmine went to take a shower so she would be ready to play outside with Holly. Shawn printed the downloaded

pictures and gave them to Anu who
was working in the backyard.

Anu gasped when she saw in some
of the pictures a tall, slim man wearing a
red-checkered shirt and sitting on a bench.
He looked a lot like Joseph. She showed
the pictures to Darshan who had just come
down and was ready to leave for his clinic.

Darshan confirmed that the man with
the red-checkered shirt was indeed Joseph. He
had a good acumen for remembering people.
It was part of his profession and Joseph had
come to the clinic for treatment a few times.

Anu gathered the pictures saying,
"I'll let Detective Tracer know about
Shawn's discovery and show him the slips
of paper and these telltale pictures on
Monday when I go to the station. You never
know. Maybe they have significance."

Her husband left for the clinic and Anu
hurried to finish her yard work. Both Darshan
and Anu were good at gardening and enjoyed
working outdoor. They firmly believed in
the ancient dictum "If you want to be happy
for an hour, do feasting; if you want to be
happy for a day, get married; however, if you
want to be happy forever, do gardening."

This year, Darshan had planted
tomatoes, green peppers and cucumber
plants that were flourishing well. The
recent rains had been beneficial.

Anu picked the ripe vegetables, as well
as some green chilies and lemons. She also
cut bunches of herbs and lettuce leaves.
She noted that the potted pants needed
watering. She watered the herbs and then
switched the water to the vegetable garden.
She looked at her fruit trees. The apricot

and loquats had given bumper harvest in early spring. The orange trees had a lot of fruit already. The grapevine needed to be pruned. She made a note to herself to remind the gardener when he came on Monday.

She walked to the front of the house to look at the succulents. The cactus garden needed no watering. The flowerbeds were in full bloom, with roses dominating the scene.

Free from her gardening duties, Anu started reflecting over the information brought by Shawn to the breakfast table. She was sure that a perfectly reasonable explanation would be available for the fax message. Kids, she thought, have a way of running wild with their imaginations. Everything for them is a mystery and a thriller. However, Gloria's murder still continued to bother her.

Boris had said that Gloria without

fail locked the door behind her when she entered the store in the mornings. Then why was the door unlocked? Was Dr. Pearson connected to the murder? It seemed very unlikely. Dr. Pearson was an outstanding citizen, respected by the community for his erudition and gracious nature. How could he be connected with such a dastardly crime as the murder of a poor defenseless charwoman? It did not make sense to her.

CHAPTER 10

A Nocturnal Adventure

A nu, Shawn and Jasmine returned home from their Bhangra dance practice around six in the evening. Darshan was already home from his clinic and barbecuing chicken and corn for dinner.

Events of the last few days had Anu worried. She had looked closer at the pictures the kids had downloaded the day before. One shot in particular of the backside of the museum was highly intriguing and in sharp contrast to the current information that Joseph had disappeared.

In a corner of the yard, one could clearly make out a tall, thin dark skin man wearing a red-checkered shirt and sitting on a bench near a stack of wooden crates. Even from that far distance, the man bore a remarkably close resemblance to Joseph. Anu had seen Joseph at the museum on a couple of occasions when she had accompanied Shawn and Jasmine on the field trips organized by their school. Joseph would be standing at the door and handing out information brochures.

"Mom, we'll be inside in a second," said Shawn. "We're talking to Holly and Jordan."

Anu nodded and waved to Shawn in acknowledgement as she entered the house.

"How was the clinic?" she asked Darshan. She was pleased to see that he had already started the dinner preparation.

"Today was busy," he said.

"Dinner will be ready soon."

"Thank you!" said Anu. "I am exhausted.
I need to rest and revive my spirits. Somehow,
that murder in the bookstore keeps circulating
in my mind and system. I am beginning
to imagine things." She quickly set the
table and called everyone for dinner.

After they had eaten, Darshan locked
the doors and the tired couple went to bed
early after giving clear instructions to Shawn
and Jasmine to go to sleep by ten thirty.

Shawn and Jasmine were glad when
they finally saw their parents' bedroom
lights turn off at nine thirty. They knew
their parents were done for the day.

At ten thirty, Shawn, Jasmine, Holly
and Jordan met in the backyard. Earlier in the

evening, all four had taken their bikes out of their garages and hid them behind the hedge so that they did not wake up their parents when they went out. Shawn's curiosity about the fax message and other related events of the day had started to run wild. He had, therefore, planned with his friends to go to the museum after dark and fish for more information.

Shawn and Jordan were apprehensive about the girls accompanying them on this mission. Jordan tried again to reason with them. "This is a dangerous undertaking. I will be more comfortable if both of you stay home."

"Well!" said Jasmine loudly. "That's an extremely sexist statement. If you leave us behind, then we will have no option but to tell everyone that you both are off to the museum. Trust me, you'll get caught before you've gone halfway."

"Shh," said Shawn. "Okay, you can come along, but you have to be quiet and follow instructions."

The group reached the museum without any incident. All was quiet. The gate was wide open, and there was no light except the street light. The group came to a halt at a prudent distance from the museum.

"Let's pile our bicycles against the wall behind the bushes," said Jordan. They left their bicycles stacked against the wall and walked up the path to the gate.

As the group neared the gate, they saw two spooky-looking florescent kites fluttering at the museum's entrance. They heard a far-off sound of an approaching truck and instinctively ran into the guardhouse to hide. The guardhouse had no door, just a table and a chair. There was a musty stench as the place had not been in use for a long time. The offensive smell was a combination of mildew, dead leaves, rotting wood and dust. All four of the children were scared and huddled close to each other, wishing they were back at home in their warm, cozy beds.

Shawn saw a moving beam of light and signaled everyone to be quiet. The children were awestruck with raw dread. Hearts racing and barely breathing, the kids crouched lower and tighter in the small wooden shelter to avoid detection. The two flickering fluorescent kites hovering on either side of the gate were also successfully doing their part in accentuating their fright. Jasmine and Holly were in jitters and huddled closer to the boys, seeking protection. All four of them were overcome with remorse and regretted that they had been willful and foolhardy enough to venture out at such a late hour. Shawn placed a protective arm around Jasmine and cautioned her to be quiet.

The truck was now quite close. It stopped right at the gate. The frightened children heard a command: "Boxes are in the shed. Take away everything. Nothing is to be stored here for some time." Shawn recognized the voice as that of Dr. Ernest Pearson.

"Okay, get going. There's no time to waste. It's all Joseph's fault." Shawn easily recognized the heavily accented voice. It belonged to Karl, whom he had met previously at the museum.

To add to the bad luck of the four frightened children, a spider chose that very moment to crawl over Jasmine's leg. Jasmine cried out with a bloodcurdling scream. Suddenly, the bright beams of the flashlights

turned to the guardhouse, which exposed
the four terrified, wide-eyed children.

"Who are you?" demanded a menacing
voice. "And what are you doing here so late?"

By now, Jasmine had completely lost her
nerve and had started crying uncontrollably.
"I'm scared. Oh, I want to go home." Shawn
placed his arm around her again to calm
her down and to stop her from crying.

The driver of the truck panicked at
the commotion created by discovery of the
children. He reversed the truck and started to
back away. The man with the angry voice ran
after the truck, waving his flashlight. "Hey!" he
shouted. "Where are you going? Come back!"

The truck roared away.

"These are the kids from the
museum!" exclaimed Karl angrily in his thick
European accent. "I remember them."

The other angry man was still standing down the road, glaring after the truck. The children could make out his profile in the middle of the road.

A man entered the guardhouse, and the kids recognized him as Dr. Ernest Pearson, the curator of the museum. Dr. Pearson also recognized the kids. He tuned to them and gently demanded an explanation for their presence. "Why are you here so late and alone?"

Shawn had regained his composure. Keeping his voice intentionally low, he replied, "We're lost. We were riding our bikes, racing each other, and suddenly we lost our bearings. Then we saw the museum and made it to this booth, thinking it was a phone booth. It was so dark, and we noticed the spooky kites fluttering at the gate. It looked eerie. Then we saw two beams of light moving towards us and we lost our nerve."

"We have been away from home for some time, and our parents are missing us by now," said Jordan, keeping up with Shawn's story. "Maybe they'll be here soon, searching for us."

"I'm scared!" screamed Jasmine deliriously. "I want to go home. Call my mommy and daddy!" Tears pouring down her face, Jasmine continued shrieking.

Dr. Pearson bent down to console little Jasmine. She grew more scared and had another outburst, sending out a shower of saliva and tears. Dr. Pearson retreated hastily, wiping the sticky droplets from his face. Jasmine's cries seemed to throw the three men into a frenzy.

"For Pete's sake, be quiet!" hissed Karl. "I hate children. They drive me up a wall. Be quiet!"

The angry man who had just returned after running in a vain attempt to catch the truck said, "We need to get rid of them. These children are too nosy."

Dr. Pearson took him away from the guardhouse and said, "Joseph, don't blow your top. You have already done enough damage by your unwarranted intrusion into the Gloria affair. I had admonished you to leave Gloria alone. All she wanted was money, and I would have given her enough to check out of Mayhaven. Now keep your hat on. Police will be trampling all over the place if anything happens to these children."

"Sir, you know that I've taken care of you since you were two years old. I love you like my own son. I do not want anyone to interefere with your plans and ruin your glorious work in any way."

"That is why Joseph I advise you to leave the kids alone," emphasized Dr. Pearson.

Dr. Pearson then came back to where children were in the guardhouse, oblivious of the fact that the children had heard every word of the conversation and now were extremely anxious to get away. He spoke to the children gently in an effort to mollify them, especially Jasmine. "I should contact your parents. What number should I call?"

Shawn knew that his mom and dad would be very angry when they learned their children were out so late. But he was now more scared of Karl and Joseph. He readily cooperated and gave the phone number.

CHAPTER 11

Meeting at Midnight

Darshan and Anu were thunderstruck when they got the phone call at midnight from Dr. Pearson. They immediately called Diana and Steven Akers and all of them rushed to the museum.

Dr. Ernest Pearson was waiting at the museum gate with the children. They loaded all four bikes in one van and the children in the other. They then profusely thanked Dr. Pearson and drove back home.

The parents were extremely furious at their children for leaving the house after dark and without the knowledge and permission of their parents. They reminded the kids that danger lurked everywhere. There are muggers, kidnappers, slave traders and ransom seekers ready to grab an unwary child or even an adult. It is always better to be safe than sorry.

Having vented their anger, the group settled down in the family room where Anu served light refreshments. Everyone was high strung, looking at Jasmine's tearful dust-laden face, wondering if this was for real or just a dream. They wanted to understand the logic behind their kids going out on this nocturnal adventure without telling them first.

Soon the reality sank in. "Thank God the children are safe," said Diana. Her words seemed to have a soothing effect, and the tension in the room started melting, letting people breathe more easily.

"I cannot believe you children had the audacity to go to the museum all by yourself, this late at night, without letting us know," said Darshan. "You could have got seriously hurt. Thank God Dr. Pearson and his hardworking staff were still there and called us."

"Dad, I am very sorry but I felt this was the only way to find out the truth," Shawn took the lead to offer an explanation. "We told you about the fax message that I found in the museum, but you wouldn't put much value on it. Anyway, all this was my idea. I talked Jordan into this. Holly and Jasmine came to know about the plan and threatened that they would tell you if we didn't include them too. I'm sorry I didn't ask your permission, but I knew it would not be granted."

Turnig to his findings during the evening, Shawn added, "Dr. Pearson is really not all that great, as everyone makes him out to be. There is something fishy going on at the museum. Joseph was there too. Didn't Detective Tracer say that Joseph had disappeared? Joseph most probably killed Gloria."

Shawn's premise was received with full attention. The Singhs and the Akers were stunned at the news that Joseph might have killed Gloria.

Then Shawn, Jasmine, Holly and Jordan recounted the events of the evening. Everyone listened with rapt attention.

Anu said, "It is strange that Dr. Pearson should deliberately say that Joseph had disappeared while he was still hanging around him." From a drawer she pulled out

the pictures that Shawn and Jasmine had
printed earlier in the day. She passed the
prints around to Darshan, Steven and Diana.
"Look at these. They were taken by Jasmine
at the museum. What do you think?"

She singled out a picture and
showed it to Diana and Steven. "Does
that person looks like Joseph?"

Everyone closely examined the
pictures and agreed that even in such long
shots the person in the picture definately
bore resemblence to Joseph. Darshan
decided to call Detective Edward Tracer.
"I think we should call Eddy and let him
know what you sleuths have uncovered."
He winked at the four children which
brought smile to everyone's face.

Darshan called the detective
at his residence telling him what

the kids had stumbled upon at the
museum. Detective Tracer responded
that he was coming right over.

Detective Tracer dressed immediately
and left to meet the Singh's. On the way, he
radioed the Mayhaven police headquarters
breifing them on the situation. He requested for
a unit to be dispatched to the museum just to
keep a watch. He also requested for a back up
squad to be kept ready for possible police raid.

Detective Edward Tracer was surprised
to find that the Akers were also present at
the Singh residence. He listened carefully
to Darshan and Anu, especially about the
miniature sculpture on the key ring and its
resemblance to the mask in the museum.
He examined the pictures and asked the
kids to recount all the events of that night.

The children told him about the

incidents that took place at the museum including their encounter with Dr. Ernest Pearson, the fax message, mesage on the paper in the trash basket, the boxes piled behind the museum, Dr. Pearson's new associate named Karl Sorley and the pictures. Shawn and Jordan also went over the details of their adventure that night.

Detective Tracer listened carefully and then immediately called his station to give a go ahead orders to the waiting squad. "There is something fishy going on at Mayhaven's World Discovery Museum. Head there with full police backup. I will be there in twenty minutes."

He turned to the group and said, "Good heavens! I think I know what's going on. I don't yet know how it is connected to Gloria's murder, but we'll find out." Detective Tracer then thanked the Singh and the Akers families for their prompt action in informing him and then extended an invitation to the whole group. "Well, would you be interested in observing some real police action from a safe distance?"

"Yes!" said all the four children in unison, looking to their parents for permission.

Anu expressed agreement. "It's already well past midnight. Nobody is going to get much sleep anyway. We might as well see how the story wraps up."

Detective Tracer let the kids ride in the police car and the parents followed in their own vehicles. In less than ten minutes, everyone was back at the museum. The place was in utter chaos. Police cars were everywhere with sirens blaring and red lights flashing. Floodlights and flashlights were shining everywhere.

The kids remained in the car

and watched as Dr. Pearson, Joseph
and Karl were marched handcuffed
towards the waiting police vehicles.

"Thank you and well done," Detective
Tracer said briskly a few minutes later.
"You are a very brave but foolhardy group
of boys and girls. You have helped us
nail a highly complex case in record time.
Now go on home and get some rest."

He then turned to the parents and
asked if he could have the whole group gather
in his office the next day around noon.

Bhangra is a traditional Indian folk dance known for its robust movements and pulsating music.

CHAPTER 12

Pieces Fall into Place

Sunday newspapers in Mayhaven had gone wild over the story of the tempest that had broken loose at midnight at Mayhaven's World Discovery Museum. Every newspaper was vying with the others to display photographs of Jasmine, Shawn, Holly and Jordan in the police car as prominently as possible on their front pages. Side by side, there were also photographs of Dr. Ernest Pearson, Joseph and Karl being led to the waiting police cars. It was

the same situation with all the television
and radio news channels. The "Brave Group
of Four," the nickname bestowed upon the
four friends by a doting community, was
in ecstasy at their heaven-sent moment of
glory. The group was relishing every bit of
adulation showered upon it by the media.

"I don't remember anybody taking
our photos at the museum last night,"
said Jasmine happily looking at the
picture of them in the police car on
the front page of the newspaper.

"Hey, we are famous!" called out
Holly, grabbing the paper from Jasmine.
"They got all of us in the picture. We
are all staring out the window."

"I think this picture was taken when
we were watching Dr. Pearson and the rest of
the gang being escorted out of the building,

into the police cars," said Shawn, who had walked over to look at the newspaper. "We were fortunate to have the ringside view."

The Singh and the Akers families had just returned from breakfast at "My Very Own Pancake House". The idea was to relax and release some of the tension of the past twelve hours. They had had a stately meal of pancakes, eggs, orange juice, milk and coffee.

Later in the day, the two families drove down to the Mayhaven police headquarters to keep their afternoon appointment with Detective Tracer. The detective met them in front of the police station and escorted them to Chief Daren Hall's office. The chief was busy on the phone. He motioned for them to come in and sit down. He had already seen to it that there were enough chairs in the room.

The chief put the phone down and

turned to the children. "Well done boys and girls. Your efforts have been a big help to resolve this baffling case. The pictures taken by Jasmine provided us with valuable pieces of clinching evidence. Thank you once again for your invaluable service to the community.

"But personally, I am bewildered about whether you deserve a reward for bravery or a reproof for foolhardiness. There is no point in disregarding the element of personal safety at any time. Unwittingly, you strayed into the underworld realm of crooks, criminals and gangsters. Even hardened officers on our force fear venturing out on such missions without proper backup. Remember, your time is precious. Use it judiciously to study and expand your knowledge. Concentrate on your curricula and be equipped to go further in life. Go by the maxim 'Never trouble trouble, unless trouble troubles

you.' Never put your precious life in peril."

The parents added their voices in assent

to the sensible advice handed out by the chief.

The chief then systematically unfolded

the story of the crime. "Gloria was a poor

self-effacing domestic worker. Dr. Pearson

is fabulously rich, gracious and giving.

No one in his wildest imagination could

have thought that a person like Dr. Ernest

Pearson would have ever anything to do

with a despicable crime like murdering a

decrepit old maid. Appearances, however,

are invariably deceptive. Dr. Pearson is fired

with the zeal to do more and amass more.

Unfortunately, hunger for riches is never

satiated. The more you get, the more you covet.

"Dr. Pearson is a distinguished

academician and a leading professional in

the field of period antiques. This field is a particular preserve of the wealthy. The trade in art is dazzling but has its sinister side too. The lure of fabulous gains has promoted the underworld to step in and grab a bigger piece of the action. Their activities range from robbing museums, art galleries and private collections to blatant plundering of tombs, temples and churches, not to mention defrauding of insurance companies. The more audacious pursuits involve illegal excavations at prominent historic sites and unauthorized removal of the excavated materials. The other links in this chain relate to activities like smuggling the looted objects across national frontiers, furnishing fake identity documentation and hiking prices through rigged auction sales."

The chief paused for a moment.

Everyone was glued to his speech when he continued. "After their disappearance, the art objects have to be stashed away for an extended period until the public outcry about the heist has died down. Dr. Pearson has considerable warehousing capacity at his disposal, which is ideal from the viewpoint of the illegitimate dealers in antique art. After all, Mayhaven is a small community located on a sea front close to the Mexican border, conveniently hidden from prying eyes. Dr. Pearson's place has considerable advantage for the dealers in clandestine goods. The new activity at the museum of organizing special exhibitions by taking articles on temporary loan from sister museums, came in handy as a good cover for haulage of containers of all sizes routed to and fro from the museum."

"Who would have imagined that Dr.

Pearson was such a crook hiding behind his mask of gentility and graciousness," observed Dr. Darshan Singh. "Maybe he was also tempted by the consideration that he would get to look at a piece prior to its entry in the market and could use the opportunity to make the first bid to acquire it at a more affordable price."

"You are correct, and that is how it started, and somehow ended with Gloria's murder," said Chief Halls. "If it had not been for her murder, we would never be investigating Dr. Pearson and his affairs. Detective Tracer can share with you the story in detail, as he has been in charge of the investigation."

Detective Tracer then narrated a summary of his investigations to the attentive group. "You are right, Darshan, Dr. Pearson had received a tempting offer from an art dealer for storage of his payloads on the museum's premises on a long-term basis. Dr. Pearson had accepted the offer because of the fabulous sums it would bring as rent."

"Well, it is really true then that Dr. Pearson is obsessed with the subject of ancient history as revealed through antique art," remarked Diana Akers. "Most likely in his mind he was doing the right thing."

"Being much cheaper, the smuggled works had been eliciting Dr. Pearson's attention for quite some time," added Detective Tracer. "He has already amassed a sizeable stack of vases, statues, icons, ancient pottery, coins, bronze figurines..."

"But where does Gloria fit into all this?" asked Anu impatiently.

"I am coming to that," said Detective

Tracer. "Stashing of stolen goods is a felony in itself. Gloria had somehow gotten wise to it. Well, as the saying goes, still waters run deep. Once our simple, guileless Gloria realized the bizarre activities going on at the museum, she became a blackmailer."

"To begin with, Gloria started blackmailing Dr. Pearson in a small way. But with time, she became bolder and started raising the price of her silence. Dr. Pearson got vexed with her manipulations and offered her a generous settlement that would allow her to leave Mayhaven for good. She seemed to be willing, as she was eager to return to her native Mexico. But the negotiations came to an abrupt standstill on an issue that had never been in reckoning at any time previously.

"Gloria was a staunch devotee of Saint Francis. During her daily chores of

cleaning the museum, she had come upon
an idol of Saint Francis lying encased in a
box in the basement. In her mind, she was
certainly convinced that the idol was the
same one that had been reported missing
from a major cathedral in Mexico. The idol
was valued at around fifty thousand dollars.
She told Dr. Pearson she wanted to return
the idol to the church herself. Naturally,
Dr. Pearson feared that the open return of
the statue to the cathedral by him or Gloria
could draw attention to his activities."

Continuing the account the detective
said, "Dr. Pearson did not fancy himself to
belong to the class of notorious purveyors of
stolen art. In his mind, he takes himself to be
a caretaker or a veritable savior of the precious
relics of the past, which otherwise could
have been lost in the hands of an untrained

person. The carriers and thieves of such objects generally lack training in handling and protecting these precious possessions from atmospheric corrosion and damage from improper handling during transit. Then there is the aspect of their proper cataloging, as well as recording of their authentic lineage, without which these would be lost irretrievably. So, in a way, Dr. Pearson was providing a much-needed service towards preservation of our heritage. Our people will be using powerful magnifying glasses to go through the documentation we have seized from the museum to sift the real from the fake."

Detective Tracer continued his narrative. "On the night preceding the murder, both Joseph and Karl had heard furious arguments between Dr. Pearson and Gloria. The meeting ended with Gloria shouting at the top of her voice that either she got the Saint Francis, or she would be going to the police. The choice was his. Dr. Pearson was calm and betting upon the eventuality that Gloria would see reason and ultimately come around. But Joseph and Karl had their own calculations.

"Joseph has been in the employment of Pearson's for a long time and is devoted to the family, especially Dr. Pearson, with an intensity bordering on fanaticism," said the chief. "On the other hand, Karl Sorley, the new associate at the museum, is a hardened criminal who is already on the run from law. He came to Mayhaven not only to keep an eye on the smuggled consignments as they moved in and out of the town but also because he could live in hiding here for a while."

"No wonder Karl flinched and became annoyed when Jasmine took a picture," interjected Anu.

"The day of the murder, Joseph went to visit Gloria early in the morning. He knew that Gloria worked part-time in the morning at Kanega Books and Music," the detective said. "Gloria knew Joseph and let him in the store. Joseph argued with Gloria that it was a lousy idea for her to go to police. He offered to intercede on her behalf and persuade Dr. Pearson to give her a more generous settlement. She actually agreed to wait for some time for the new offer. Joseph left the store and related this to Dr. Pearson, who immediately came to the store to offer a large sum of money in exchange for her leaving Mayhaven permanently on that very day."

"So Joseph did not kill Gloria," said Shawn, who had been following the story intently.

"Right! We were all under the false impression that Joseph or Dr. Pearson had something to do with Gloria's murder. However, it was Karl Sorley. Karl had actually stolen Dr. Pearson's revolver a couple of weeks ago because, as they say, when push came to shove, he wanted to be ready. He took the gun with him that morning when he saw Joseph leave the house early in the morning. He saw Joseph go into Kanega Books and Music store and heard the two of them arguing. He was sure that Gloria was going to go to the police. As soon as Joseph left, Karl walked into the store. Gloria must have heard the door bell ring and seen Karl. She knew that Karl was bad news and ran to the back of the store to get away from him. Karl followed her, shot her point blank and left. The noise of the gunshot got masked by the thunder in the sky. Karl then strolled to the lake and

where he dropped the revolver into the lake.

"When we arrested Karl, he denied

involvement with everything," continued

the detective. "But as soon as we identified

him as the French national that the FBI was

looking for, he became very cooperative. He

is wanted in France for an array of crimes.

Anyway, Karl has confessed to the murder and

the FBI is looking for the gun in the lake."

"All is well that ends well!" said the chief

rounding off the session. "Bad guys in prison,

good guys on the street. Congratulations,

kids. The station has decided to honor

you by awarding you junior sheriff badges.

However, I still stand by my words. This is

no time for young and budding souls like you

to stray into the crappy arena of crooks and

racketeers. Your primary concern for now

should be completing your education with distinction. Subsequently, if you want to take up police work as your chosen careers, our door will stand open without any reserve.

The four friends stood and shook hands with the chief as he pinned the junior sheriff badges on their jackets one by one.

Book Order Coupon

Mail in this order coupon and start your collection of "The Singh Family Series".

Please send "Mystery at the Bookstore" at the following address:

Name: _____

Ship Address: _____

_____

_____

Email Address: _____

Phone Number: _____

1. One Book = $ 10.00
Sales Tax Included.
2. Shipping and Handling (S&H)
Shipping and Handling (US only) =$ 5.00 first book and $2.00 for additional books.
Shipping and handling (outside US) = $ 9.00 for first book and $5.00 for additional books.
4. Total per book (book price+S&H)=X= $

5. Total number of Books (n)= _____

6. Total Order =   Xn = $ _____

Make check payable to Booksmart Publications.

Mail this order form and check to:

Booksmart Publications
PO Box 4774
Dept. B
Mission Viejo
California 92690
For more information email b_smart@cox.net or
Leena@booksmartpublications.com.
Visit www.booksmartpublications.com